THE
BODIES
OF
THE
ANCIENTS

The Books of the Dissenters by Lydia Millet

THE FIRES BENEATH THE SEA
THE SHIMMERS IN THE NIGHT

THE
BODIES
OF
THE
ANCIENTS

a novel

The Third Book of the Dissenters

LYDIA MILLET

Big Mouth House

Easthampton, MA

The Bodies of the Ancients copyright © 2017 by Lydia Millet (lydiamillet.net). All rights reserved.
Cover art © 2017 Sharon McGill (sharonmcgill.net). All rights reserved.

Big Mouth House
150 Pleasant Street #306
Easthampton, MA 01027
info@smallbeerpress.com
smallbeerpress.com
weightlessbooks.com

Distributed to the trade by Consortium.

First Printing
January 2017

Library of Congress Control Number on file.

ISBN: 9781618731289 (trade cloth); 9781618731296 (ebook)

Text set in Minion Pro.
Printed on 50# Natures Natural 30% PCR Recycled Paper in the USA.

For Beatrix Heard

One

It was June again on Cape Cod and the summer crowds were trickling back in. The beaches wouldn't be mobbed till July, but families from Boston were already starting to flock to the roadside seafood restaurants. From behind the smudged and scratched-up pane of the school-bus window, Jax gazed at them. They were willing to wait long periods of time for a table; some of the grown-ups looked at their phones, and a few ran around after their kids, but most of them did nothing much other than stare out into space, baking in teh sun and breathing exhaust fumes. All for the sake of eating a fried-fish sandwich.

Jax shook his head.

Maybe they were hollows, he said to himself. Maybe they were mindless zombies waiting to be consumed by flame.

June meant school wasn't out yet but felt like it should be, because going to classes was kind of a joke once everyone switched into summer mode. Since the beach-going tourists brought the work, some of the older kids' jobs had already started. The beachgoers were also the restaurant-goers and the gas-station customers and the only people who *ever* bought the paintings in the art galleries (paintings of docks and water and boats) or the hand-carved duck decoys and lobster-shaped jello molds in the gift shops.

Grown-ups resented the tourists more than kids did, Jax thought. Kids saw the crowds as a chance to make spending money, not an irritation. Plus, when the tourist season came, there was just more life around the Cape's towns and beaches. More things *happened*.

Anyway, he and Cub were good at ignoring crowds. Jax had to be, thanks to his mind-reading hobby/curse. He was better at shutting it off than he had been when he was ten. These days it was pretty easy to lock down the noise of thought traffic and float above it, feel almost as free as he imagined his sister and brother did, not able to read minds at all. He never pinged by accident anymore.

And Cub, well, he'd never had trouble ignoring the rest of humanity. He came by it honestly, like his parents before him—card-carrying dweebazoids. All three of them were more interested in science than other people.

The two boys walked around in a bubble most of the time. They didn't talk to anyone else and no one else talked to them—so that now, on the long backseat of the bus, they didn't even have to lower their voices while they spoke right out loud about stuff Cub claimed should probably be encrypted.

That was the "beauty of social anonymity," according to Cub. He embraced his nerd identity. He said it was a mass movement these days. Empowering. And Jax—well, Jax got along with other kids fine, if they deigned to talk to him. Which most of them didn't.

No one cared about two gangly eleven-year-olds, one with glasses, braces, and a long nose, the other, well—him, Jax. He didn't embody *geek* the way Cub did, being a kind of average-looking kid with blond hair and blue eyes, but inside he had to admit he was way weirder than Cub would ever be.

And he had his own ways of disappearing.

As the bus turned off Route 6 and bumped along a quiet, potholed road headed for Jax's neighborhood, Cub sat beside him on the seat with his giant pack on his back. (The pack was so big Cub could barely squeeze into the seat with it, but it never seemed to occur to him to slip it off.) He stared down at his phone, where the screen was scrolling through a bunch of scraggly lines that looked like heart-monitoring equipment or maybe radio signals.

Jax had no idea what Cub was working on right at the moment—he wouldn't ping him, of course, that was a given. And he usually didn't ask directly either. Cub's explanations were long and pretty boring. It was probably something to do with SETI, the Search for Extraterrestrial Intelligence, because life on other planets was Cub's obsession of choice. Some people said SETI had gone out of style in the '90s, when the government stopped paying for the research program, but Cub passionately disagreed.

He claimed ET stood for "Eternal Truth."

When Cub started a conversation with an Earthgirl, or really *any* kid who wasn't Jax, he only had one topic. "Do you have any idea how statistically unlikely it is that we're the *only* life-forms in the *universe?*"

If the girl in question didn't instantly walk away (rare), he'd start droning on about the Drake Equation while she fumbled in her locker or her eyes darted around, looking for a friend to perform a daring rescue.

"In fact, the probability that there are *abundant* alien life forms in other solar systems is extremely high! The only variable known with any degree of certainty is the rate of stellar formation in the galaxy. Call that rate R. . . ."

Jax was known in his family for long, complicated explanations, but at least he shut up when people told him to. Cub didn't even hear them speak in the first place.

Despite his obsession, or maybe because of it, Cub insisted the Cold One couldn't be of extraterrestrial origin. He didn't believe the Carbon War was about ETs taking over the Earth.

It was preposterous, he said.

Sure, he believed there were life-forms sprinkled throughout the universe in probable abundance . . . but that didn't mean they'd ever make it *here*. Or even try to. They were too many thousands of light-years away, across billions of solar systems or even billions of galaxies. There was too much space between the stars.

The Cold was just a plain old Earth native, Cub had assured Jax on multiple occasions. A bad guy, sure, but hardly a bona fide alien.

When Jax asked him why the Cold was trying to transform the climate, if he'd evolved here in the first place, Cub had a number of explanations ready. From being a species that lived under the floor of the ocean, the Cold One was trying to colonize the surface. And global warming had already been happening, so he just piggybacked on that.

Jax didn't argue over the alien origin issue. Maybe it didn't really matter where the enemy came from, after all. The point was, he was here. Now.

"Earth to Cub! You receiving?"

"Yes, I heard you," said Cub, still staring at his phone screen. Something Jax had said about five minutes before was hanging in the air; Cub hadn't gotten around to answering. "You're saying these 'air elementals' aren't *exactly* a threat to us, like the Pouring Man or the Burners?"

"Right. Not personally."

"Because they're *gases*? In the air?"

"Yeah, greenhouse gases, according to what I've been discovering," nodded Jax. "So what we call greenhouse gases are the Cold One's air elementals. He didn't create them, like the Pouring Man or the Burners—he just uses them. And they don't take a humanoid form at all—they're just the mostly invisible emissions from burning fossil fuels that are heating up the atmosphere. I mean they're actually *more* dangerous than the Pouring Man or the Burners— just not to us *individually*. To us they might look like black or gray smoke, I think, sometimes. But mostly we don't see them."

"How about the last kind of elementals. There's a fourth kind, isn't there?" asked Cub. "*Earth* elementals?"

He raised his phone and without warning snapped a pic of Jax's face, one of his more startling habits. Jax blinked, briefly blinded by the flash.

"You mean, what form do earth elementals take?"

"Yeah, Jax, that's what I mean."

Cub manipulated Jax's picture and assigned it to a contact list. He was constantly updating his files, almost compulsively; he didn't like to have a contact picture for Jax that was more than a week old. His glasses were so smudged it was hard to believe he could even see through them.

"So those ones I don't know about yet. My research hasn't really . . . showed me them."

Actually his research had showed him plenty this week, and what he'd found out had shocked him.

But he wasn't mentioning that to Cub.

"Now, *my* research is going quite well," said Cub self-importantly. "Evolving data analysis on the distributed computing project . . ."

Jax looked out the bus's window at the houses blurring past, white and brick with orange lilies in their front yards. Then he leaned his head against the tinted Plexiglas and closed his eyes. There was a flash of sound and words when he let down his guard, before he brought up the thick, soft screen he used for relaxing—the usual flash of other minds' thoughts, in this case the rest of the kids on the bus. He heard and felt quick snatches of *That's stupid* (a sharp jab) and *Why's she being so mean?* (a tremble at the edge of tears) and then something from the driver, sadder: . . . *say melanoma is aggressive. . . .*

But it passed after a couple of seconds: he moved his screen safely into place like a sliding door in a groove. Click.

He let out a sigh of relief.

What he'd been shocked by the day before had been something he'd learned about his brother, Max. Jax and Cara had always assumed Max didn't have a special talent—that unlike them, Max, good-looking and confident and popular, was a regular person. That among his many advantages in life (Jax had always worshiped Max, and he was man enough to admit it), their older brother *didn't* count any outlandish old-way abilities like mindreading or mindtalking or vision.

But yesterday Jax had mastered a new mental trick where he could push himself into the Web, push his mind into sectors of hypertext as though they were 3D spaces, without any need for passwords or other permissions, without the tech savvy of someone like Cub. (Cara thought Jax was a computer whiz, but he wasn't. He had the basics, that was all—nothing compared to Cub, who'd apparently been born knowing Linux and C and HTML and learned the rest as a toddler.)

It was like digging through digital space, through plunging depths of data and structures of code, and he could feel or glimpse bits of content the way he saw and knew other things he wasn't supposed to—the landscapes of other minds, hidden spaces to travel through, pieces of history stashed in the old ones' library. It was so exciting at first that he turned and plowed around in a bunch of different directions, "willy-nilly" as his dad would say.

He didn't even have to use the keyboard, except for resting two fingers on the touchpad.

At first he hadn't paid attention to his surroundings in detail—he'd felt like some kind of underground burrowing animal beneath the root system of a massive old tree, exploring a maze of branching tunnels and burrows. Maybe he was blind like a mole or deaf like a snake and moved by sensing vibrations through a network that went down deep and narrow . . . though to be honest it didn't feel *organic*, like dirt and tree roots and bugs, but more like a circuit diagram he moved along, pushing himself along the lines to the boxes. Or like a diagram of a family tree, he thought.

But almost as soon as he was getting a sense of the geography, *almost* as soon as he got over the weirdness of this delving, this forking off in direction after direction, feeling at once buried and like he had undiscovered countries at the edge of his perception, he bumped into something that was familiar and strange at once. Like a rock in his path that tripped him and then turned out not to be a rock at all.

He hadn't meant to spy, not this time—he'd promised his brother and sister not to sneak into their heads without asking, and it was a point of pride to honor that agreement. But this wasn't Max's head, it was just Max's email—where, without trying to, Jax had found out something he hadn't asked to know.

His big brother had a secret.

It had been Hayley's idea for Cara to practice in the back room of her mother's hair salon.

The storeroom was stocked with shelves and shelves of bottles of hair dye and, in front of them, yellowing paper cards holding swatches of fake hair. The hair came in all the colors of the rainbow, from browns and golds to purple and green. There were jars full of blue liquid that hairbrushes had been submerged in since the Dawn of Man; there were different styles of wigs sitting on creepy foam heads. (The lips and eyes of the heads had slashes of red and blue across them, which Hayley had crayoned there long ago. Judging from the level of skill, she must have been about three.) There were white-wicker laundry hampers full of towels and the snap-on black smocks the customers wore over their clothes when they were getting their hair done; there was a chair with metal legs and a peeling plastic cushion patterned with faded pink flowers.

Against a cinderblock wall was a washer/drier and an old pedestal sink, stained a rusty brown around its drain. The only window was small and square and always open, with filmy polyester curtains that flapped and rippled in the breeze (carrying in just the faintest smell of the ocean). On the wall was an old calendar with pictures of kittens on it and a screen door that opened onto a patch of concrete and weeds.

Behind the concrete and weeds was a tall hedge, a scrubby field of blueberry bushes, and the paved bike path Cara loved. It ran for miles in a gentle curve along the green forests and ponds and cliffs of the national seashore.

"No one will *ever* bother you in here," Hayley had promised, sticking small glitter stars onto her fingernails. "I mean my mom grabs the laundry hampers like once a week, but most of what she needs is already up front. So you'll have plenty of privacy."

Except for Hayley herself, of course, who stayed to chat for a good fifteen minutes every time she came in to get a tube or bottle, and sometimes actually perched on top of the washing machine while it was shaking around. Wearing short-shorts that Cara's father said would get her arrested in some countries, she liked to pull her skinny legs up and draw on her knees with a ballpoint pen (hearts with faces, her name in fancy writing) while she delivered long monologues involving school gossip or the sordid love lives of pop stars.

Cara needed peace and quiet for what she was working on, and it could be hard to get enough of that at home. Her old-way talent was vision, a minor talent compared to the amazing abilities her little brother had. But it was a talent all the same. Recently her mother had been helping her learn how to call up visions without the help of artifacts—without the tools she'd had to rely on in the beginning. The evil-eye ring she'd used to see things far away had been stolen; she'd had to return the book she'd once stepped through to get to places halfway across the world. So now she was working on calling up sights without those objects of talent.

And she had to concentrate so hard, when she tried to summon, that the smallest thing could derail her—including their new puppy whining at her bedroom door. Max had brought the puppy home from the no-kill shelter where he volunteered, and they were all pretty obsessed with him. He was a curly haired, floppy-eared yellow mutt they didn't have a name for yet and kept on calling Puppy.

But the real news in the house wasn't Puppy. It was their mother.

She'd finally come home.

True: she had to be away a lot, and she still hadn't told their father what was going on. Instead she'd made the kids promise to keep that genie in the bottle for a little longer. And when it came to their father, as far as Cara knew, her mom must have simply persuaded him to trust her. (Cara suspected he was so relieved to have her back that he was probably willing to wait as long as she wanted for a full explanation of why she'd been gone.) She'd told him just that it had to do with her family of origin—some relatives their father didn't know. She'd said those relatives were in trouble, and she'd had to go help them; she'd said it wasn't over, either, and that she might be called away again.

But it wouldn't be for as long, if she could help it, and he should know she'd always head home in the end.

The kids were relieved at the change that had come over their father. For one thing, he slept in his own room again, the room he shared with their mother—where he was *supposed* to sleep, instead of the ratty couch in his study where he'd crashed almost every night for the months she was away. And he was sleeping normally again, instead of in restless fits and starts. He didn't stalk through the house in the small hours of the morning anymore.

And he looked ten years younger. At least.

He'd never been much of a hugger, having kind of an old-fashioned, formal way of carrying himself, in his suit and vest with the watch fob hanging out of a special small pocket. But since their mother came home he'd got into the habit of suddenly hugging them. He did it in a solemn, deliberate way: he'd show up in Cara's room and enfold her silently in his arms for an awkwardly long time. Finally he'd drop his arms and shuffle out again, back to his cluttered desk and scholarly work.

He did the same thing to Jax and Max—and, of course, to their mom.

It was actually more comfortable to see him the way he'd always been, distracted and hunched over his academic papers, than to fall prey to one of his long, earnest hugs.

Even though Cara's mother didn't have the vision talent herself, she knew how to teach it. They had to have the sessions when Professor Sykes was out of the house, since he didn't know anything about the old ways or the Carbon War. Or, say, the fact that his wife moonlighted as a sea otter. And sometimes a fat-lipped fish.

To summon you had to clear your mind and then do what the old-ways people called *gives*—you had to give yourself up each time you wanted a vision. You had to drop all your defenses and be perfectly open to the world. Her mother said it was like what some poet had called "negative capability"—being everyone and no one at once.

But you had to clear your mind first, and that was almost harder. Mind-clearing was like meditation, which some people worked all their lives to get good at.

She'd chosen her first summoning one time after she'd spent two nights on a biology project about shorebirds. Her mother had told her to ask to see something tranquil, so she asked for a view of bank swallows in Nova Scotia. And after a silent, doubting moment where nothing happened at all, into the afternoon dimness of her parents' bedroom had come the birds and their landscape. There was the water of the Atlantic, there was a narrow beach and short cliffs, and there were the birds: slight shadows dipping over the water, then fluttering up to holes in the sand bank and disappearing inside.

When you were first learning to summon, you were supposed to ask for visions outside your own life, scenes that wouldn't be of direct use to you and were unlikely to hurt you either. You had to establish a trust with the old language, her mom had said, the way a woodcarver might establish trust with his knife. Sometimes she'd stare at a candle; sometimes she scanned her body, beginning at the feet and relaxing each part of it till she got to her head. Other times she just breathed very slowly and concentrated. That took forever, though. It was an incredibly delicate balancing act to keep from getting distracted.

How hard you tried was a huge part of vision. Her mother had said to her once, talking about her own job as a marine biologist, that it wasn't how smart you were on paper. It was how you used your mind that counted.

So she'd decided her vision gift was small but precious, like a snow globe.

Thus far she hadn't summoned without her mother right there in the room with her, coaching. But after she saw her mom and Jax at the table—both with their deep abilities, their talents that she could only think of as a kind of magic—she suddenly felt determined. She wanted to show them both she could master her vision and use it to help. And no matter how minor that was (compared to Jax, who had so many old-ways talents no one knew where they ended, and her mother, who could send thoughts into people's heads and take the shape of animals), it would be real and it would mean something.

So here she was, at Hayley's mother's hair salon, where Hayley worked three days a week after school and every day in summer. Swim team was over for the year—all the extracurricular teams and clubs were done with. Only a couple of exams were left, math and Spanish.

Today was her trial run. Today she was going to try to summon a vision related to the war, though not directly. A minor vision, a tiny piece of the puzzle—so small it couldn't hurt.

"OMG that Pitbull guy is *so* ugly! His outfits rock, though," burst out Hayley, sticking her head in the door.

"Hay! Come *on*. I needed an hour all by myself, remember? With no interruptions?"

"I like his music OK too," said Hayley. "When he takes off his shades, though, you see why he always wears them. It's like, Oh snap. Face fail."

Maybe coming here hadn't been the best idea, thought Cara. She'd wanted it to work out, and she'd wanted to keep her friend company on the bus and at the salon—she thought she could do both. But trying to keep Hayley from talking was like trying to stop a tidal wave with a bucket.

Cara was sick of not making progress. She needed to find a place of solitude.

The *dunes*, she thought.

She loved the dunes.

She could ride the bus up to a lonely landscape of protected dunes on the national seashore, the stretch of sandhills and valleys called the Province Lands that you could get to from Route 6. The pulloff was just before you got to P-town; maybe Max could drive her there. She'd get dropped off and hike in as though she was headed for the beach, but then veer off into the parts none of the beachgoers bothered to explore. In those quiet yellow hills she'd finally be alone, where the wind blew over the beachgrass and goldenrod, and scrubby bushes grew in the shady dips between the ridges.

"Even Marc *Anthony's* cuter than Pitbull," reflected Haley, "though he's a grandpa too. Obviously."

"Seriously, Hay, let me try to have one sight. Leave me alone for another half hour, at least, and then we can get a soda from the vending machine before I head home. OK?"

"OK, OK," said Hayley, fiddling with an earring. "Just one more thing before I go: something *so weird* happened out there on the floor? One of the clients, this super-old lady, who I just thought was a regular Islander, started talking in a, like, foreign language! My mom and I were the only ones there and she starts basically speaking in tongues. We were like, Uh, *sorry?* So finally she stopped, but it was freaky. Do you think she's demented? Or is she *possessed?*"

"Because she speaks another language?"

"Well, I mean, speaking it to *me*. Obviously *I'm* not from a foreign country."

"Hay. I *have* to practice now. OK?"

"Fine! Anyway. You're not fun currently."

Once the door shut behind Hayley she took a deep breath and sat down on the flowered chair. She turned on a small fan on the shelf beside her, whose wire cage was festooned with soft tendrils of dust that rose into the air like streamers when the blades started whirring.

This morning she'd heard her mother and Jax talking about the Navy—something about submarines near the Mid-Atlantic Ridge. The ridge, a huge mountain range that ran north and south beneath the ocean, was also the closest they'd ever come to pinpointing the Cold One. She hadn't been able to ask them to explain because her dad had joined them in the kitchen, humming an ancient song that went *Hang down your head, Tom Dooley*. When he broke off singing he started talking to her mom about an article he'd written that some dusty journal was going to publish. "The piece on self-crucifixion in the Philippines, as you may recall, dear, is out for peer review. Meanwhile—"

She and Jax had busied themselves with the blender, dumping bananas and cocoa powder into milk for a smoothie. Their father was standing just a little way along the counter, fiddling with one of the knobs on the toaster oven—which made Jax cautious about saying anything to her that might capture his attention.

"Of course, as a form of devotion, the Church tends to frown on self-crucifixion . . ." their father had murmured. He opened the toaster oven door and slid out his toast. "Dang nab it! Already burnt. I just don't have the knack of this high-tech gizmo."

"Dad?" said Jax. "It's not a cutting-edge form of new technology. It's a *toaster*."

"What were you saying about the deep ocean?" Cara asked him, under her breath. "Did you find out something?"

"Looks like the Navy has a connection to our old friend Roger," he said softly.

"And?"

"We found an email thread that had been encrypted and then . . . see, the Atlantic Fleet does some weapons testing and big training exercises nearer the continental shelf, but suddenly it looks like at least one submarine in that fleet is headed really far out. Toward the middle of the ocean—toward the ridge. *Near the coordinates of the source*."

Their dad loomed over them with a worried expression. Cara felt the bottom fall out of her stomach.

"Kids. What am I doing wrong?"

"Wrong?" asked Cara.

Did he mean, why wouldn't anyone tell him anything? Why was he left out of the loop? Why was he alone in their family without even knowing it?

"I mean the toast gets black every time! Do I have the dial set wrong?"

Relief.

"Here. I'll show you," she offered.

"Where's Max?" asked her mother, jiggling a frying pan and flipping an omelet.

Max was seventeen now and already working two jobs for the summer, one on a fishing boat and the other at the expensive restaurant where he'd worked for two summers. His junior year was almost done; he had only one exam left (and a bunch of year-end parties).

"On the boat already," said Jax. "He left at four-thirty this morning."

"Ouch," said their father, beaming at Cara as she adjusted the toaster oven for him and slid in a fresh, unburned slice of bread.

She and Jax hadn't had another chance to talk that morning before they got on the bus for school and sat with their separate friends, but she'd been thinking all day about what he'd said. What did it mean, a U.S. Navy submarine heading for the Cold's stronghold? Because if the Navy was in league with Roger—wasn't that what Jax had said?—then they wouldn't be *attacking* the Cold. Would they?

Roger was the same man who'd spied on her mother for years and then tried to poison Jax; he couldn't possibly have turned against his master.

She didn't understand, but it alarmed her, this idea that the whole *military* could be on the other side.

She decided it couldn't wait. She called Jax's cell.

"Can you finish what you were saying this morning? About the submarine?"

"Wait a sec, I'm just getting off the bus . . . yeah, see ya, Cub. OK. So at first we didn't really know what we were seeing, because they use all this jargon and code and stuff, and some of it's hard to get into. And then, when we *did* think we understood what they were saying, and I mean, this was like at two in the morning—"

"You guys were up doing stuff at two in the *morning*?"

She stood up, pacing back and forth across the supply room. It felt stuffy and hot. She pushed her face up close to the dusty fan to catch a breeze.

"—we could hardly believe it. We're still not a hundred percent, which is why Mom hasn't called you or Max yet to bring you up to speed. But it *looks* like someone there is collaborating with Roger and others like him, and it may not be official but it's some powerful admiral dude, Mom says, who's high up in the Navy and his specialty is nuclear materials, like nuclear reactors and nuclear weapons and stuff. And I guess there's an old nuclear warhead his guys found beneath the Atlantic, way out in the middle of the ocean near Bermuda. In the Bermuda Triangle! It was lost under the ocean in the Cold War, in 1986, when this Russian nuclear submarine called *K-219* exploded and later sank to the Abyssal Plain, like 18,000 feet deep. Most of the 34 warheads it was carrying broke when it sank, which sucked because plutonium leaked out—"

"Jax. Slow down."

"Anyway. I guess one of the warheads was secretly reclaimed recently by this admiral guy, and now he has a top-secret plan to actually . . . *use* it. Use the warhead."

"Use it—how?"

"Mom and her friends think this admiral, and his mini-strike force, intend to use the bomb on a target in the rift valley. The Mid-Atlantic Ridge. Where the Cold pumps out his carbon pollution. His methane holes, all that."

"I don't get it. Are you saying the Navy's on *our* side? And but they're trying to, like, take out the Cold with a nuclear *bomb* . . . ?"

"Uh, no," said Jax. "Sorry. I'm afraid not." He sounded fifty years old sometimes. "We don't think they're on our side at all."

"Then what?"

"We think they're kind of like support staff for the Cold. Our working theory is—it's Mom's, at least, and some of the other old-ways leaders—they're trying to trigger the great carbon release."

"You mean—release of greenhouse gas?"

"We think they're working with the Cold, and he's gotten impatient. In his reverse-terraform—that's what Cub calls it. You know Cub: he gets everything either from science or sci-fi. Anyway. Mom says she's afraid the Cold wants the atmosphere change to happen not over the next twenty or thirty years, but now."

Cara sat down on the flowery chair again.

"So the plan, as we're understanding it so far, is to use this warhead to break open whatever the gas reservoir is and let out—a lot of it. At once."

"We can't stop the Navy from dropping a bomb, Jax," she said after a minute. "I mean—we're just a couple of kids. . . . We can't do *that*."

On the other end, she heard background noise as Jax went into their house—the slam of a door, Puppy barking.

"Mother wants us to meet tonight," said Jax, whispering now. "I guess Dad's going to be out of the house, so we can speak freely. He's going for a moonlight paddle with that other history prof from 4 C's, you know, whatshisname, the guy with hair that sticks right out of his nostrils?"

"Nose Rapunzel?"

She choked out a giggle in spite of herself. It had cracked her up so much when Max said that.

"Yeah. Dad said this guy's been bugging him to do a paddle for years, and he finally had to break down and say yes, so they're doing it—a night kayak in the marshes at Fort Hill. So we'll have the house to ourselves. Max has to work the dinner shift, so it'll be after."

"OK," she whispered back.

There was no reason for her to whisper. But still she was whispering.

After she hung up she sat without moving. It was too overwhelming to think about bombs, so she decided to focus on summoning. She still had another half-hour before she had to ride her bike home for dinner.

What could she ask to see?

She had to stay safe, her mother had said. But it couldn't hurt to summon the sight of someone on *their* side of the war. Could it? Someone good, someone helpful. She concentrated and tried to clear her mind, thinking of the massive, flying creature that had come to her rescue once, hers and Hayley's and their friend Jaye's . . . oops. Now she was off on a distracting tangent, stuck thinking about Jaye, whose parents had decided to go on sabbatical back in January and had taken Jaye away until next fall. She missed Jaye, though they Skyped and texted some-times. . . . Q, her mother had told her, was the creature's name, a healer and a helper, something like that. Q was ancient.

Where was Q now?

Maybe it was the nagging thought about Jaye, how much she missed her, and a guilty feeling that they hadn't Skyped more in the past month or two—nagging feelings like guilt were the worst when she was trying to mind-clear—but she was having trouble getting clarity. Thoughts clung to her like burs, and all she could summon was the front room in the salon, the space on the other side of the same wall she was looking at. There were Mrs. Moore and Hayley arguing, as Mrs. M popped her gum and teased an older lady's hair into a weird shape that sat on the top of her head like a squirrel.

Cara sighed disappointedly but kept her eyes closed as the scene unfurled inside her eyelids. She'd confused what she was asking for, probably, but it was still a vision—technically it was still amazing she could do this, she reminded herself. Right? A wall was still a wall. And seeing through it without even using her eyes was already more than most people could do. OK, so it wasn't what she'd tried for, but at least it was a summoning.

It would have been funny to see the two of them, arguing in their typical blunt way over the fact that Hayley wanted more piercings in her ears, if it hadn't also been a bit of a fail. The vision even came with a soundtrack, which they didn't always.

"Six*teen*?" said Hayley. "I know a girl with multiple piercings who's only in sixth grade! And one of the piercings is in her *nose!*"

"The better to lead her around on a ring by, I guess," said Mrs. M in her Southern drawl, and shook her head. To the lady whose hair she was puffing up, she said: "And here I thought only *bulls* had rings in their noses."

"In numerous African cultures, girls under puberty are allowed to stretch their earlobes down to their shoulders," Hayley informed her mother scornfully. She seemed to be reading the line off her phone.

"How nice for them," said Mrs. M. "You want to move to Africa, honey?"

"I'm just saying," persisted Hayley. "A little multiple ear piercing is *nothing*."

The dunes, Cara told herself, as the scene faded and she opened her eyes. She stuffed her own phone back into her pack and slipped on her shades.

⚏

Jax found his brother rummaging in the bathroom cupboard. As he hesitated outside the open bathroom door Max grabbed onto what he wanted and pulled it out roughly, not bothering to untangle its long snarl of electrical cord.

"Is that mom's hair dryer?" asked Jax.

OK, so dumb question.

"Yeah, man," said Max, turning and brushing past him and down the hall, holding the blow-dryer in one hand like a fat plastic gun. Its plug bounced along the floorboards. "I'm all about the hair these days."

Jax followed Max into his bedroom, where his favorite skateboard, with fire and skulls painted on it, lay on the messed-up bed.

"You're going to blow-dry your skull board?"

"I gotta replace the grip tape on this baby," said Max. "See? Already took the truck bolts out. If you warm up the old tape it's easier to peel off."

Jax sat down beside the board on Max's bed, watching, and soon Max was moving the dryer steadily over the top of his board. They couldn't talk over the noise, so Jax waited till his brother shut the dryer off again and started quietly peeling.

"So you know," started Jax nervously, "I promised not to ping you guys without asking. And I haven't."

"You *better* not," said Max.

"I haven't, I haven't," Jax reassured him. "But there's this other thing that happened by mistake."

"This *other* thing?" Max turned and looked at him over his shoulder, flicking his wrist to dislodge a piece of peeled-off tape from his fingers. "What kind of thing?"

"It was an accident," said Jax. "I have this new deal, see, that Mom's been helping me with, where I can kind of, like, access cyberspace without hacking or having to know passwords. . . . I can kind of move through, you know, just mentally, some of its volumes of data. . . ."

His brother stopped peeling tape and looked at him, curious.

"And so the first time I did that, see, I wasn't completely in control, and—totally by accident, I swear!—I ended up close to home and I saw an email I shouldn't have. An email that I fully know wasn't my business."

Max waited, his face not showing much of anything. Jax felt so anxious he was almost queasy.

"And it, uh, I was surprised, because it was a message to you from Mr. Sabin."

Jax actually squeezed his eyes shut and hunched his shoulders, waiting for Max's anger. He couldn't stand it when his brother was mad at him. Even when he deserved it—in fact it was worse then.

But Max didn't say anything. Instead, after a few seconds Jax heard the blow-dryer start again, and when he opened his eyes Max was calmly waving it over the next section of tape.

"Aren't you pissed at me?" he asked, the next time his brother flicked the switch and set the dryer down.

Carefully pulling up a long strip of tape, Max shrugged.

"Nah," he said finally. "I'd have told you eventually."

"So—is it OK for us to talk about?"

"Just between you and me?"

"Whatever you say. Sure."

"I needed to get advice from someone outside the family. I didn't feel like . . ."

He stopped, searching for words.

"I didn't know what it was at first. And I felt cut off from—I got in touch with Sabin because I liked him, you know, I met him at the Institute that time we went with Cara. And he was pretty nice to me. I felt like I could trust him, to talk to. If I talked to Mom, say, and then it turned out I didn't have any talent at all—I just didn't want it to look like I was desperate to . . . to be *like* you two. Well, you *three*. If I was wrong, and what was going on with me was just a fluke and not an old-way deal at all, I didn't want to look like the guy who's trying too hard to fit in."

"For sure," said Jax. "I get that."

Usually Max didn't admit this kind of thing to him.

"Because I was OK with *not* being like you guys too. In a way I wanted to, like . . ."

He looked up, holding his board across his lap.

"I wanted to keep Dad company. By *not* having a talent. Being outside of this."

"I understand," said Jax. And he did.

Max began peeling tape again.

"I'd been wondering about that prophecy last August, whether I was even *in* it. It talked about the three of us diving down to the shipwreck? Remember?"

"Of *course*," said Jax. As though he ever had the luxury of forgetting anything. "It called us 'interpreter, arbiter, and visionary.'"

"Only it was *Hayley* who went, in the end, not me, after I crashed the car and had to stay in the hospital. I mean we assumed it was by accident that she ended up there. But maybe it wasn't. Maybe that's how it was always *supposed* to be. You're the interpreter, being a brainiac, and Cara's the visionary, and maybe Hayley was always the arbiter. She *did* have to judge something, right? Decide which of you—you two—was real? So I thought, maybe Hayley was always *meant* to be the 'arbiter.' Maybe it was her all along."

"It's possible," allowed Jax.

"Which would mean, well, maybe there isn't much of a place in this war thing for me."

"But now—?" asked Jax slowly.

"Sabin says what I have is faintly related to Cara's ability. And to some of yours too. Except it's different."

"I didn't see anything in that email except for that you *have* an old way," said Jax. "And Sabin knew about it."

"When you were a hollow, when the Cold had you, Cara was supposed to use Mom's memory to get you back, right?"

Jax didn't like to be reminded. The way he thought of it now—the time when he'd been hollowed out and held in limbo to be used by the Cold—well, it wasn't like any of his other memories. Instead of details, what came to him was usually a wave of nausea, a wave of despair.

He didn't answer in time, so Max went on.

"My talent, or whatever, hinges on memory too. It works by memory, Sabin said."

He started the dryer again, holding his other hand up to signal *just a minute*. When its annoying high *wheeeesh* died down he bent over his tape.

"But how'd you find out you could do this thing? And I mean—what *is* it?" asked Jax.

Outside Max's bedroom window the sky was turning into evening, and small lights on the pier twinkled through the silhouetted branches of a pine tree. *You're a pest*, Max had said just last week. It was the tone that hurt, though. Jax had been standing too close, and Max always got cranky when he felt penned in—especially if it was Jax doing the penning. Jax had felt a hot burn of shame when he said it. He'd promised himself not to do anything to make Max talk to him like that again.

He got off the bed hastily and strolled to the window, where he stuck his hands way down into his pants pockets, pushing down on the fabric bottoms of the pockets with balled-up fists. He gazed out at the twinkling lights.

Max labored over his board and kept on talking.

"See, I had this raggedy old hoodie of Zee's, but it used to be her favorite, and I was trying to figure out if I should bother getting it back to her," said Max.

Zee'd been his girlfriend for a while, and before that his good friend, and now he wasn't supposed to even see her. They were fairly sure she was involved in the war, whether or not it was her own fault—and not on their side, sadly.

"So I was holding it, and I was thinking about her, and all of a sudden I felt this pain in my—right here."

He tapped his forehead with a forefinger.

"And then instead of standing there beside my locker, I was walking down this street—Zee's street—and Jax. I was *her*."

"You were *her*?"

"I was looking out of her eyes and feeling her feelings. I was in her body, not just her head. Is that what it feels like when you—you know. Ping?"

"No," said Jax slowly, "that's not a ping."

"Jax, seriously. It was *scary* at first. Man."

"Wow," said Jax.

"All that was left of me was a tiny, fly-size speck of consciousness. A fly on the wall. And for a good couple of minutes—but it felt like a lifetime—I felt what it was like to be Zee. It was—it's hard to explain. But among other stuff, it was confusing and weird. She wasn't—she's so sad."

"That's a high-order old way for sure," Jax told him. "I don't know of anyone else who can do that."

"I don't know," said Max. "It was kind of paralyzing. Like I couldn't *talk* to her. She didn't even know I was there. So she had—she had no privacy. I was just *her*. And I didn't ask for it."

"Welcome to my world," said Jax. "I didn't ask for any of my . . . skills. Either."

"And it really hurts my head too. It gives me a *killer* headache, dude. Afterward I was popping headache pills for the whole next day and drinking water and all that and no matter what I did, it didn't stop my head from throbbing."

"Do you *have* to be touching something that belongs to the other person?"

"Sabin said it probably just makes it easier. The way using an artifact did for Cara. It's like a hunting dog with a scent, right? Those dogs like something to sniff to get them started. So now I'm a hound dog. Great."

He tore the last of the old tape off his board and ripped some new tape off its cardboard packaging. It looked like black sandpaper.

"I want to keep this under wraps for now, Jax. Just you and me. I mean I don't know what it *is* yet. It's only happened once after that first time. And it *hurts* when it happens. I don't want to have to do it if I don't want. I don't want to have to *use* it. Not till I know how to control it."

"Sure," said Jax.

Normally he didn't like keeping major secrets from his family any more than Max did. But it wasn't often there was a secret that belonged to just Max and him.

"I don't want Mom and Cara *on* me about it. For now, I just want to leave it be. You can live with that, right?"

"Sure. Yeah. It's your deal."

Max was sanding the deck of the board now and seemed intent on his task, so Jax decided to go. Max ignoring him was often his cue to leave.

Headed down the stairs he searched his mental archives for anything he might have encountered about this old-way talent, mentally scanning the pages he'd recently looked at. His photographic memory came in handy sometimes, though not as often as people thought.

After a minute or two, by which time he was raiding a box of cookies in the kitchen cupboard, he found a reference. EMPATHS, he brought up on a page in a thick Institute volume that had recently been digitized, and stopped with a chocolate-chip cookie halfway to his mouth. The talent was rare, the entry read. He scanned further. Empaths had the gift of putting themselves in other people's shoes, "moving beyond the emotional experience of sympathy to *feeling-with*," was what the text said. "Transfer of mind-gestalt into another subject." He'd bet that was what this was.

He'd bet that Max's talent was an extreme, old-way version of empathy.

Who would ever have guessed?

He thought of all the times his older brother had snapped at him or made him feel even smaller than he was, and he wondered.

Just because we have a talent, he decided, doesn't mean we always use it.

Two

It was getting near to sunset when Cara and Jax stood on the front porch eating popsicles and Max helped their father tie his two kayaks onto the top of the car. They were so long the tips stuck out past the front and the back of the Subie.

Puppy, with a line clipped to his new harness, didn't want to stay on the porch and kept straining on the leash, which Cara was gripping desperately with her non-popsicle hand. Puppy was strong. He dragged Cara down the steps and halfway across the yard before Cara gave up and distracted him by letting him lick the remains of her popsicle.

"OK," said their dad finally, "water, snacks, headlamps, check. I better go. I'm already late."

They watched him get into the car and rattle down the road, waving his hand out the open window as he went.

Now, thought Cara, *now* she was going to find out what was really going on. Her mother was hunkered down in her bedroom and had told them to come join her once their father was on his way.

"Cara!"

It was Hayley, yelling from her own yard.

Argh. Cara jogged over with Puppy bounding beside her, Dumbo-style ears flopping.

"Is it happening?" asked Hayley when Cara reached her. Puppy sniffed around her feet avidly.

"Yeah, like now," said Cara.

"Can I come? I want to hear what's going on too."

Cara wasn't sure how her mother would answer that. She hesitated; Puppy kept sniffing Hayley's feet.

"Come on! Why not?" begged Hayley.

"What will you tell *your* mom?" hedged Cara.

"Mom!" yelled Hayley, right into Cara's ear.

Her mother appeared at the front door, a magazine curled in her hand, and pushed open the screen.

"Uh-huh? Oh hey there, Cara honey."

Immediately Puppy leapt into the air and pulled Cara toward Mrs. M.

"Can I go over to Cara's house for a while?"

"Is it OK with her mama?"

"Of *course* it is!" said Hayley before Cara could answer.

Puppy was going berserk, sniffing so hard around Mrs. M's feet that Cara was afraid his face would seize up. Then he started whining, and before Cara knew it he was actually *peeing.*

Peeing right next to Mrs. M's high heels and bright-pink toenails. Like inches away.

"I'm *so* sorry!" she said. She was so embarrassed she was probably blushing. "He's not trained yet."

"Oh, it's all right," said Mrs. M. (Awl *raht.*) "I just *adore* puppies. What a cutie. What's his name?"

She leaned down and rubbed behind his ears; Puppy flopped flat on his back and lay still, legs hanging limply.

"We don't have one yet," said Cara. "Lame, huh."

"How about Elvis? Elvis is *perfect* for him!"

"Um . . ."

"Mom. Why would they name him *Elvis*? No one thinks about Elvis Presley anymore. Like seriously, no one. He's Paleolithic, Mom. People have barely *heard* of him. Except you. The last Elvis fangirl. Let's *go*," said Hayley, and grabbed Cara's leash arm.

"But he's the *king*," protested Mrs. M softly, as they pulled Puppy away with them.

So it was four of them that trooped up to the attic clutching the last popsicles from the box, Puppy loping so close at Hayley's heels Cara was afraid he would get stepped on. The door was closed, but Max didn't bother to knock before he pushed it open.

"Well hello, Hayley," said their mom, and spun around in her desk chair.

"Hey, Mrs. Sykes. I made Cara let me come. I can hear what's going on too, can't I?"

Mrs. Sykes looked solemn.

"If you take it seriously, yes. These are grave matters, Hayley."

"You're not kidding!" said Hayley. "I was there, remember? I've been burned, Mrs. S. It took me two months to grow back my eyebrows. People, like, laughed at me."

"I know you have," said Cara's mother, and softened. "I know."

Behind her, Cara saw, her mom's large widescreen monitor displayed a map with ridges on it—the kind that showed the shape of mountains and the depth of valleys. Before she could figure out more it was replaced by a screensaver, the old-school kind with colorful fish wiggling across a fake aquarium.

"Are we going to have to do something? Like fight more of those elementals?" asked Hayley, sounding half-eager, half-frightened.

"Not exactly," said Cara's mom. "Go ahead and sit down… you can toss your dripping sticks in the trash can. There you go. Take the bed, go on. And the rocking chair."

Before she had a chance to say any more—as Max took the chair and the other three, plus Puppy, settled on the bed, Hayley plumping pillows behind her head—Jax spoke up.

"Mom, I've been wondering what the fourth elementals are," he said. "The earth elementals. Is he—the Cold—is he going to deploy them too? Or is the next play just about that broken arrow?"

"Broken arrow?" asked Max.

"Lost nuclear weapon," said Jax.

"We'll get to that," said their mother, and stood up from her desk chair to pace back and forth, looking graceful as ever in a long, flowing skirt. She twisted her black hair into a bun behind her head and stuck a pen through it. "The elementals aren't our direct concern right now. Air and earth aren't embodied the way water and fire were. And of course, they both existed before he started using them. But they're far more important than the Burners or the one you called the Pouring Man. They make those guys look like Lego villains."

"Super," said Hayley. "That's great to hear."

"But earth and air aren't elementals we face as direct opponents. Air elementals are the gaseous products of combustion, like carbon dioxide and methane and nitrous oxide. And they're doing the work of warming the climate for him. There are far, far more of them since he began his work of dirty industry. But earth—earth elementals are very old indeed. And there are fewer and fewer of them, because they're the basis of his carbon revolution. The elementals of earth, you see, are the substances that produce these gases for him. And for us. Not all, but most of them."

"The *fuels*?" asked Jax.

Their mother nodded. "What we call fossil fuels. Yes."

Cara looked at Jax. He was nodding excitedly.

"Of course! That's what the volumes I read were talking about! I didn't make the connection! *The bodies of the ancients*. That's what it said."

"Bodies?" asked Max. He was picking at a scab on his knee.

"You know—that's why they call them *fossil* fuels," said Jax, switching to lecture mode. "Oil and natural gas are made out of the really small bodies of ancient animals and plants. Zooplankton, algae—that stuff. And coal too—well, coal's mostly just from plants. All of them got covered and compressed and heated up and carbonized over millions of years. And their—remains stayed buried in the Earth until we started digging them out and burned them."

"Some on our side," added their mother, "some of us with a more—how should I put it? Mystical? Or spiritual?—way of thinking believe that was a deep insult. A kind of crime. They believe the earth elementals being used like this is a desecration of the ancestors."

"Get out," said Max. "An insult to dead algae? Like algae would give a crap?"

Their mother smiled lightly and shrugged. "The point is that these ancient bodies, the earth elementals, are the Cold's force for transformation. We're not equipped to face them right now. Our mission is with a whole different enemy."

No one said anything for a minute. Then:

"Fabulous," said Hayley. "A *new* monster?"

"*What rough beast slouches towards Bethlehem to be born?*" asked Max.

Nice, thought Cara, my big brother's waxing poetic while picking at knee scabs.

"*Yeats*, Max?" asked their mother, smiling a little. "You branching out from Shakespeare?"

"It was mandatory. We had to memorize 'The Second Coming' in English."

"Well. It's a little more complicated than a monster. It's people."

"People," echoed Jax.

Their mom told them all what Cara and Jax already knew, about the renegade admiral in the U.S. Navy and his Russian nuclear warhead.

"*Mom*," said Max, when she had finished, in his most cutting tone. "You're not seriously suggesting that we, the Sykes family of Wellfleet, Massachusetts, plus the ditzy blond girl next door—"

"Hey!" interrupted Hayley, bouncing up off her cushions indignantly. "Sexist! Major sexist alert!"

"—take on a bunch of guys with nukes?"

"Well," said their mother, sitting down in her chair again and spinning back to her computer screen, "we won't take them on *alone*."

She touched a key and the fish screensaver vanished, replaced by the map. The kids got up and went to look over her shoulders. She zoomed out and around the map until the up-close lines and numbers disappeared into the shape of the Atlantic Ocean; then she zoomed out farther to reveal more and more landmasses, marked North America, Europe, Africa. As they watched, it morphed from pastel colors with black writing on them into a photorealistic Earth with real-looking colors, brown and drab green and yellow and blue-gray, like a satellite view on Google.

It was some interface Cara had never seen before.

She watched as night fell across the world, zone after zone winking into darkness. She could still see the shapes of the continents, though; beneath the moving sleeve of dark she recognized the shapes of the Great Lakes, for instance, like three fronds of a palm tree dangling over the middle of the continent. But as the dark fell, small lights winked on: first slowly, then faster, until they were uncountable suddenly, sprinkled across the continents. The coastlines merged into blots of light where the big cities were.

"This is us," said her mother softly.

"Who?" asked Max.

"*Our* army."

Cara gazed at the spider web of white dots twinkling like stars on the black-velvet background. It was beautiful. She wondered how many of the dots were shapeshifters like her mom, mindtalkers like Mrs. Omotoso or Mr. Sabin from the Institute. How many were like Jax, like her? Or just regular kids? Like Max and Hayley?

"Thousand points of light, Mom?" said Max.

"Let me show you," said their mother, and clicked on one of them. It was a dot the size of a pinprick, blinking out in the middle of the ocean, near the bottom of a landmass Cara thought might be Greenland. Or Iceland. She always got them confused.

Then they were zooming in, in, in on it, at a dizzying pace—her eyes hurt if she tried to keep the screen in focus. It was like using the windowleaf, the feeling she'd had falling through its open pages, hurtling through space. The screen had that same uncanny quality, meaning it had to be old-way technology too. The zooming accelerated, like they were on a roller coaster.

Not normal.

"I feel pukey," said Hayley. "OMG."

"3D without the glasses," said Max, admiring.

And then they stopped zooming in and were looking at a different darkness, something softer that moved a bit, glinting.

"More light," said Cara's mother softly, and the darkness lightened a notch—like going from midnight to dusk. It was water, waves gently peaking and falling, and beneath it a dark shape swam. Oval. With flippers. They followed behind it as it came up for air, then dove under again—but not far under.

"Is it—is it a turtle? The leatherback?" said Cara.

"Ananda!" said Jax.

"That's so *cool*," said Cara.

She'd never thought she'd see the ancient sea turtle again. It had been almost a year. And last time she'd seen her, the turtle had been hovering in a big, slightly too-slimy tank at the Woods Hole aquarium.

"Is that the turtle you guys told me about? That Jax talked to all mentally?" asked Hayley, pushing Cara aside so she could lean in and see.

"Did she make a jailbreak?" asked Max.

"More like, she was released for good behavior," said their mom.

"You can't tell, looking at her like this," said Max to Hayley, "but that reptile is almost *six feet long*. She's taller than you are."

"Don't call her 'that reptile' once she's listening," warned their mom.

And she reached out and tapped a single key: ENTER.

Suddenly the sea turtle stopped moving forward and moved her flippers differently, rotated to face them.

The leatherback knew they were there.

Her face was hard to make out—white spot against a gray hide, and a gray hide against the gray of the water. Her eyes looked small and black and like all sea turtles she had a small, curved beak instead of an upper lip; her great front flippers moved slowly back and forth just under the surface, and the lines of the long ridges on her back were delicate seams of white.

"Can she—can I talk to her?" asked Jax. "From here?"

"I don't know," said their mother. "*Can* you?"

"Try, try!" said Hayley, and looked at Cara. "I want to see him make the air wiggle."

"He can't," said Cara confidently. "Not long distance like that. He can't even ping from *Boston* to here. Ananda's in the middle of the ocean."

"I do have a new old way Mom's been helping me with," said Jax, and closed his eyes, leaning up to touch his fingers to the keyboard. After a second he jerked back, opening his eyes again.

"That was quick," said Max.

"It's a kind of virtual travel he's been working on," said their mother. "Hard to explain."

Max snickered. "No kidding."

"She's got all these pilot fish swimming underneath her," said Jax. "She said they tickle."

"Pretty far north for a pilot fish," muttered their mother. "Surprised they stuck with her."

"She did *not* say they tickle," said Max to Jax. "You're full of it."

Jax gazed at him with his eyes wide, blinking. It was hard to tell whether his feelings were hurt or he was just glaring.

Then their mother clicked some keys and Ananda disappeared, replaced by the nighttime map with its web of twinkling lights.

They retreated from their cluster around the computer and sat back down again.

"Anyway," said their mother, "Ananda's one among thousands. More—*tens* of thousands who are on our side."

"Huh. Are the rest of them turtles too?" asked Max.

Hayley let out a chuckle—till she saw Mrs. Sykes' face.

"All hail the turtle army!" said Max. "Raise a flipper if you're in! Turtles vs. nuclear warheads. Guess who wins?"

"Max?" said their mother coldly. "You and I will talk after the others go."

Max shrugged and flicked his knee scab onto the floor.

"Ew, ew, ew," said Hayley, and shuddered.

And she used to have a crush on him, thought Cara.

"But the answer is, obviously, no," said their mother tightly. "We're all kinds. We're people in different forms. And you kids would do well not to make too many assumptions about folks' identities. Or about what creatures of other forms are capable of. Believe *me*."

A feeling of awkwardness hung among them. Cara flashed to her elegant mother as a, well, ugly fish. Before her mom had disappeared and come back she'd always been cheerful and kind—at least, that was how Cara remembered it. Maybe a little cranky when she was tired, but always patient. But she hadn't liked it when Max made fun of Ananda. Not one bit.

Cara snuck a sidelong glance to gauge her mother's expression: her full lips were pressed into a thin line. Last time they'd gone up against the Cold it had been without their mother—mostly. Now she was here with them. An adult calling the shots.

And on the one hand, it did seem more secure this way. She trusted her mother. There were real dangers of life and death, and her mother could handle them better than any kid. Right?

At the same time she remembered how it had felt when it was just them, just her brothers and Hayley and her, taking leaps into the wild and unknown. There couldn't ever be the same excitement when they were . . . *supervised.*

Don't be a baby, she told herself. This isn't a game. It's a war. It *shouldn't* be left up to kids.

But thinking about how serious it was—that wasn't helpful either. It gave her a sinking feeling.

"Seriously," said Max. "I don't get it. If this guy's some kind of military supervillain who's stolen these old weapons and wants to use them, why don't we just expose what he's doing? Wouldn't the government, like, arrest him? In a heartbeat?"

"The Cold has a lot of well-placed friends," said their mother slowly. "In industry. In politics. We don't know all their names or capabilities. That means that if we wanted to be sure of the outcome, we'd have to go straight to the top. And while we're certainly not just a *turtle army*, we don't have direct access to the commander-in-chief. That's for sure."

"Why can't we just beam into the Oval Office while he's alone and have a chat with him? You know—through a magic book that defies the laws of physics?" asked Max.

"Nice sarcasm," said their mother. "Though you should have said *seems* to defy. Max, you know we never expose the old ways to outsiders. But just as importantly, we don't know how close the Cold has gotten to the seats of power. It could be very close."

"But how about the media? Like CNN? Or newspapers? The *New York Times*, or whatever?"

"Almost all the credible news outlets are owned by large conglomerates, as you may know, Max. And sprinkled across their boards of directors, their editorial boards and major stockholders—his allies. In the past they've cropped up in very inconvenient places. We've learned to trust no powerful institutions."

"You sound like a conspiracy-theory person."

Their mom lowered her reading glasses on her nose and fixed her gaze on him.

"Max? You can be sure of one thing. What we have here *is*, in fact, a conspiracy."

Max, who'd been leaning forward, threw his hands up and sat back in the rocking chair.

"Then tell me," he said, and this time he wasn't snarky but serious. "Why didn't your people, with all their superpowers, stop this guy a long time ago?"

"That," said their mother, "is the best question you've asked me. And the truth is, we didn't see what was happening. We knew he was here, we'd had a history with him I'll tell you about some other time. But we didn't know he wanted to colonize the surface until just a few years ago. So we didn't know he was behind the warming. The realization dawned on us . . . sadly, it dawned on us very late."

"So what's the game plan?" asked Jax.

"Well," said their mother, and her face relaxed a bit. "We have a part to play. In fact we have several. It so happens," and she swiveled in her chair, turning her back to the computer and looking straight at Cara, "that the admiral has a family. He has one child—a daughter."

"And?" said Hayley.

"And she lives on the Cape. In fact, girls, she goes to your school. And she's in your grade."

"What's her name?" said Hayley. "I know, like, everyone. Who's anyone."

"Her name is Courtney—Courtney Anderson. She transferred recently from a boarding school when the admiral moved his family here. Wait a second."

She turned back to her keyboard and typed, and the map of lights was quickly replaced by a page of photographs. They were mostly headshots of people wearing military uniforms and some others in suits and ties. She clicked on a small one in the corner: a girl with short hair and freckles.

"That kid! I *have* seen her," said Hayley, who had an excellent memory for faces. "Yeah! She's on some team . . . let me think. Field hockey! That's what it is. Because she wears the giant red things on her legs. Like, goalie pads? She's on the field hockey team. She's a jock."

"So you'll be reaching out to her, Cara and Hayley. I'll explain more in a few minutes. Jax, you and Kubler—"

"He goes by Cub now," said Jax.

"   you and Cub are going to have a little computer project. Well, maybe not so little. And Max will be helping *me*." Max brightened a bit, as though he'd been chosen for an honor guard. "So let me talk to Max first, and then I'll brief you, girls. Then Jax. OK?"

"We can't all just stay and hear about *everyone's* jobs?" asked Jax.

"It's probably best if we don't all know the details of what the others are doing," said their mom.

"Like terrorist cells?" said Max.

"Thanks for *that* loaded question," said their mother. "The truth is, this war is about information, partly. And we're more vulnerable if all our information is shared."

A moment later Cara was following Hayley and Jax down the stairs, Puppy padding after them with tail wagging. They headed for Cara's room.

"Cool that Cub's going to be included," said Jax. "Though I'm not sure what he's going to say when I ask him to take time off SETI."

"Who's Setty?" asked Hayley.

"Not a girl," said Jax.

⚎

By the time it was Cara and Hayley's turn to be briefed, Jax had disappeared into his own room and Hayley had foraged a jumbo bag of cheese popcorn, then eaten most of it—while reorganizing Cara's closet *and* having a text fight with her mother about her curfew.

When Max knocked on Cara's door she couldn't tell from his expression whether he'd gotten a serious lecture about his attitude or felt pumped for his "project."

"You two are up," he said. "Team Girl. We've got Team Grownup, Team Girl, and Team Geek."

"Nice," said Hayley.

"Yeah, I thought they were good too," said Max, and reached over to grab the near-empty bag of popcorn, which he carried away with him.

Her mom was at the computer again when she and Hayley went up to the attic, and on the screen was a face Cara knew: Mrs. Omotoso, her favorite teacher from the old-ways Institute.

"Hello, Cara. Hi there, Hayley," said Mrs. O.

"Hi!" said Cara.

"Oh, hey. You're *that* lady," said Hayley, sounding none too bright.

"Indeed," said Mrs. O. "So girls. You have a task ahead."

"Mrs. Omotoso has been researching this," said Cara's mom. "I thought I'd let her tell you about it."

"What's important to know first off," said Mrs. O, "is Courtney's a regular kid. In all your dealings with her, you're to treat her well. What her dad does, what her dad *is*, isn't her fault. I've arranged for her to be taking a test with you tomorrow—your Spanish test. She missed her own exam because of a practice, ostensibly, so she'll be doing a make-up test in the same room with you. You'll need to talk to her afterwards and find some way to be invited to her house. Text me when you've set it up."

"Talk about fast friends," said Hayley. "But oh man. There's a Spanish test *tomorrow*?"

After Hayley left, when Cara was lying in bed with her lights out, she tossed and turned. She felt—well, small. Her job was to make *friends*? That was *it*?

It had nothing to do with her vision, nothing to do with any talent she had. True—she'd barely mastered the visions anyway, so she couldn't blame her mom for not hanging their plans on *that* ability. But still. In the war over the future of the world, what *she* had to contribute was pretending to be friends with someone?

Jax was assigned the genius work, Max had been chosen as their mother's right hand, and her own mission was tagging along while Hayley exercised her popularity skills on a girl named Courtney.

❈

"Tianhe? Otherwise known as the Milky Way 2?" said Cub on the phone. Jax and his mom had stayed up way too late talking, but it was OK to call late—Cub and his family were night owls. "You're kidding, right? That thing has better security than Fort Knox. *Way* better. It has like *3 million* core processors. It's the fastest and biggest computer complex in the entire *world*. The Chinese government claims it delivers like 33.86 petaflops. Of course no one knows if that's all really true. The thing's like top-secret."

"I have no idea what any of that means, but yeah. She told me it was big."

"It's in *China*, Jax. It's *impossible*. We have less chance of hacking into that thing than meeting Dr. Who at the Wicked Oyster."

"Never say never, right?"

"Never, never, never. Never. *N-e-v-e-r*."

"Um."

"That's literally the craziest idea I've ever heard."

"Time to get crazy, then," said Jax. "Look, Cub. This is the most important job I've ever had. By far. You can put the distributed computing for SETI on the back burner for just a little while, can't you? Take on the biggest challenge of your life!"

"Craziest thing I ever heard," repeated Cub. Jax could almost see him shaking his head, pushing his glasses up his nose.

"Cub. Please. I'll owe you big-time. After this, I don't know—I'll owe you a favor. A huge one."

"Uh, yeah. I'd say so. Huge like enormous. Huge like the galaxy. Huge like the *multiverse*."

"Got it."

"Like, putting aside the virtual impossibility of breaking into the world's most secure defense supercomputer, if we get caught even trying, it's Edward Snowden time. We're talking *treason*. International law-breaking, Jackson. Plus my parents would *kill* me. You'd find me in a gutter stone *dead*."

"Well, *my* mom will thank you," said Jax. "She's trusting us with this because *no one else* can do it. I can do some things, I guess, but not like *you*. Cub, you're the only one who knows enough to do this with me."

"I can't believe your mother *wants* you to be a hacker. What is she, a criminal mastermind?"

"It's in a good cause, Cub. The best."

"That's what they all say, Jax. Before they do something crazy and illegal."

Jax waited. He was banking on Cub's curiosity. When it came to computers, unlike in the rest of his life, Cub was a risk-taker.

"You're familiar with the hacker code, aren't you?" asked Cub with a worried tone. "Hacked information has to be shared. You don't hoard it. If information is obtained, you have to open-source it. It's a matter of honor. It's right there in the code."

"Maybe later," said Jax, though he doubted it. "That can be more of, like, a long-term goal. Right now this is a war. And the first thing we have to do is get *in* there."

"I gotta take this under advisement. I gotta sleep on it. This is too big."

"Sure," said Jax. "Of course. Take till tomorrow. Sleep on it."

"Oh, that's generous. That's really nice of you. One night to make the most dangerous decision of my whole *life*."

"Cub, you're too smart not to know how important this is."

"I *said*, I'll sleep on it."

Cub hung up.

⚍⚎

Hayley had been awake into the small hours studying Spanish so she might know more words than "Ooh" and "bailando." Cara wasn't too bad at Spanish, but she still had six questions left to do on the test when she saw Courtney hand her own completed exam to the monitor.

Oh no. She'd have to leave now too if she was going to stop Courtney from disappearing—Hayley was still scratching her head over the second page. Her own test wasn't finished—and maybe worse, she'd have to think of some way to start a conversation. Meeting new people was Hayley's thing, not hers.

The classroom door clicked shut behind Courtney. Cara scrambled to pick up her backpack and race her unfinished test up to the monitor; she handed it over quickly and made for the door.

In the corridor Courtney was leaning against the wall, typing on her phone.

"Uh, hey!" called Cara as the door clicked behind her.

Courtney looked up, surprised.

"Hey," Cara went on, stumbling over her words. "You—you're on the field hockey team, aren't you?"

"Uh, I play," mumbled Courtney.

"My name's Cara," said Cara, and forced a smile. She came to a stop beside the other girl and adjusted her pack on one shoulder. "I, um, saw you wearing those big red pads on your legs." Minor lie.

"OK?" said Courtney. "And?"

"I, I just wanted to ask you what it's like," rushed Cara. "I don't know anything about field hockey. But it looks cool."

"My *leg guards* look cool?"

"Well . . ." Cara had no idea how they looked. But probably not cool, as such.

What else to say? What? What?

But then the other girl took pity on her.

"It's not the season right now," she said. "We were just messing around. So no one forgets how to hold the sticks, ha. The season's not till fall. But I used to play for Bement."

"Bement?"

"My old school."

"Oh. So—when'd you leave there?"

"Just a couple months ago," said Courtney. "Under duress."

"You didn't want to?"

"Well. All my friends are there. And I mean, I've always boarded. And this place is, like, pretty much the polar opposite of where I've always been. So."

"That's got to be hard," allowed Cara.

Save me, Hayley, she was thinking.

"So you're, uh, pretty used to boarding school?"

"I'd been there since third grade. But then my father just took me out. No warning. So yeah. Here I am."

"Nauset must be a lot different," said Cara.

She heard a voice behind them.

"I totally flunked that test," said Hayley. She came up and elbowed Cara fondly in the ribs. "You guys aced yours, I bet. Finishing early and all that."

"*You* finished early too," said Courtney.

"No, I just gave *up*," grinned Hayley. "Song lyrics only get you so far. What's your name, stranger? I'm Hayley. Cara's bff."

Cara could practically hear her own exhale—saved.

⸎

"So my parents had a really nice surprise for me at breakfast," said Cub, plunking his pack down on the locker-room bench.

They had to change for PE, which they always did in a quiet, moldy-smelling corner where no mean kids tended to roam. "I'm skipping sixth grade next year. They already talked to the school. They enrolled me in seventh."

Jax froze with his shirt over his head.

"You're kidding," he got out finally. "I thought they agreed with mine that we—I mean, then we won't be together anymore!"

"I know," said Cub glumly. "I'm bummed. I tried to argue. I even said they had an agreement with your folks about how important it is we 'have each other's support'— their words, obviously—you know. But they weren't hearing me. My dad was having a work conversation on his headset at the exact same time and just nodded and looked at me sternly. My mom said a bunch of stuff about how I wasn't 'socially integrated with this age cohort anyway,' so why hold me back. Their minds were totally made up."

A while back the school had wanted to skip Jax ahead too; in fact, they'd said he could skip *three* grades, academically. His parents had said no. They didn't believe in it; they said he would be miserable with all those older kids.

"Oh, man," was all he could muster. "That really sucks."

So he had next year, and every year after that, without Cub in his classes to look forward to. He'd be by himself. All alone.

He sat down on the bench and stared at his feet.

"But the good news, J, is that it sucks *so* bad," said Cub, "that my answer to last night's question is a resounding *yes*.

They do what they want without asking my opinion, then fine. I'm going to do the same."

"Revenge," said Jax tonelessly, and he knew he should be relieved Cub was in, but it didn't make him feel better.

"Hey, I thought you'd be way happier than that," protested Cub. "I'm risking my freedoms as an American!"

"Thanks," said Jax. "Yeah. It's a big deal. But the other thing—it's just so lame, though."

"What can I say. I'm even more bummed than you are," said Cub. "At least you have Cara. And Max. And parents who give a crap about your, like, feelings. Or whatever."

They got their gear on in silence.

❈

Hayley worked fast, Cara had to admit. Or maybe not a lot of other kids had talked to Courtney yet, because by the time they waved good-bye after the Spanish test they already had a plan for that same night—something about watching old seasons of *Project Runway*. They'd be picked up in her mother's car and go home with her. Courtney wasn't allowed to take the bus.

"They don't want me consorting with the *hoi polloi*," Courtney had said.

"Hey, me neither," Hayley'd said back. "Whatever that is, it sounds ugly."

After Courtney walked away Hayley asked, "What did she say?"

"I'll ask my friend Siri." Cara took out her phone and pressed the home button. "Siri. What's the definition of hoy polloy?"

When it came up on her screen she held it up and read it out loud. "'The working class, commoners, the masses or common people in a derogatory sense.'"

"Um, us," said Hayley.

"Yep."

"Nice. But doesn't she have to hang out with non-rich kids at school anyway?"

"Maybe the mom thinks buses are worse," shrugged Cara. "More older kids? Maybe she thinks it's not safe. I mean, it's true the driver can't stop kids from being bullied. Remember that time Jax got an earthworm put in his hair?"

"What do you think, will it be a Mercedes?" said Hayley. "A Beamer? Or a Jag? I say Mercedes. The new Jags just look like boring grampa cars."

Sure enough: the car was a white Mercedes. Courtney's mother wore a suit and had short brown hair tucked neatly behind her ears. She explained a little awkwardly as she drove them—of course Hayley had to ask right away, pretending innocence as Cara elbowed her in the backseat—that they weren't on the bus route. But as they pulled up to the house Cara noticed it was only about a five-minute walk, tops, from one of the regular stops. She knew all the stops by now.

The house was huge and right on the bluffs overlooking the bay—in fact, you could faintly see it from the shoreline behind Cara's own house, if you waded out into the marshy water a bit. Up close, she recognized it. The light flashed off it when the sun was right. It was a modern building with sharp angles and a lot of glass and light—not one of the old saltbox Cape Cods. There was a tall gate that opened automatically and a winding, paved drive. At the top of the driveway, beside the house, long grasses waved in the wind.

"Home sweet home," said Courtney as they pulled to a stop inside the big garage. Another car was already parked there, but there was room for two more.

"I'll say," said Hayley enthusiastically. "Our house looks like a trailer next to this. Oh wait—it *is* a trailer! But don't sweat it, Mrs. Anderson. It's high-end. It's a *double*-wide."

Luckily, by the time she said that, Courtney and her mother had already gotten out of the car. Mrs. Anderson had a black earpiece in and was talking as she punched numbers into an alarm pad on the garage wall.

Inside, there was a huge view of the ocean through a glass wall in the living room, which they stood at for a while, gazing. Then Courtney got bored and hurried them upstairs to her room. It was big too, with a side view of shore and ocean, and there were field-hockey trophies and framed photos of Courtney and her friends. In one picture she was standing at a goal and wearing the leg pads. Nope— not cool as such, thought Cara.

"Tell us about these girls," said Hayley, and pointed at a photo of Courtney hugging someone and smiling. "Who's this?"

"So that's my best friend, Tess," said Courtney. "Actually her aunt's friends with Tim Gunn from Parsons, that's how we got into *Runway*."

"No *way*," said Hayley. Her eyes got big and round. Cara had hardly ever seen her so impressed.

"I have all the old seasons on DVD," said Courtney. "We used to watch them on Friday nights. It was kind of a tradition. Which season do you want to watch?"

"Let's go old school," said Hayley. "Season One!"

Courtney opened a big cabinet, and there was a widescreen TV.

"Whoa," said Hayley. "You live in, like, paradise."

"Well, my mom sure doesn't think so," said Courtney as she opened a drawer of DVDs. "This place is a big come-down for her. She's used to live-in maids and the social life in DC. But I only spent Christmas there and a couple weeks in summer when I wasn't at camp. So I just miss my peeps."

Courtney ran downstairs to grab some snacks while Hayley checked out her open closet, making admiring noises about some brands Cara didn't know.

"Stop snooping," said Cara. She felt bad that they were in Courtney's house on false pretenses.

"This is an awesome gig," said Hayley. "Plus she seems actually cool. For a rich chick."

Courtney slipped back in holding bags of chips and a bottle of soda. She handed them the snacks, then kneeled down and stuck a disc in the machine.

Cara didn't mind the show, but she didn't pay much attention either. Instead she lay on her stomach on Courtney's rug—Hayley munching chips beside her and keeping up a running commentary on the different "looks" that made Courtney laugh—letting the images blur in front of her and wondering what Jax and Max were doing.

It definitely wasn't watching people bicker and design clothes.

⚏

Jax wanted to talk to his mother about what was going on, but his dad was with her in the kitchen. She held a glass of wine as she listened to the tale of last night's kayak adventure.

"So we're paddling though the marsh, and I get ahead of Steve, and then I hear him calling me. Squeaking like a mouse! Poor guy. Turns out he's dropped his paddle. The guy lost his paddle in the mud! Well, you know it's hell to back up in those oxbow channels, with the tall reeds all around—"

"Hello, Jax," said his mom brightly. "Did you have fun with Cub?

"Not so much," said Jax. But he couldn't talk about it with his dad there, so he might as well say the other thing. "Uh, so his parents are skipping him. They told him this morning. He's going into seventh grade in the fall."

Both his parents looked at him.

"Oh dear," murmured his mother.

"*What?*" said his father, annoyed. "Wait. That wasn't the

plan. I thought we all agreed."

"His mom said he's not 'integrating with his age cohort anyway,' so they're skipping him."

"Nonsense!" said his father. "He's integrated with *you!*"

"Maybe we can talk to them, honey," said his mom.

Jax shook his head. "It's a done deal. They already set it all up and registered him and everything."

"Well," said his mother after a minute. "I must say that's very disappointing."

"They could have mentioned it to us," grumbled his father. "Common courtesy."

"Well, social skills . . . ," began his mother.

". . . not their strong suit," finished his dad.

All three of them were quiet.

"Anyway," said Jax.

"I'll come up and tuck you in," said his mom.

As Jax trudged up the stairs, his father kept talking.

"I swear, that woman's on her high horse ever since they gave her the MacArthur," he said. "Next she'll be sticking the kid in Mensa."

"That poor boy will be lost among the older kids," sighed his mother. "It's hard enough for him talking to the ones his *own* age."

"Now he'll be in with the jocks, kids hitting puberty," agreed his father. "Ridiculous. You gotta feel sorry for him...."

Jax shut his bedroom door gently.

"We can be actual *friends* with her," said Hayley on the phone, when they were both back in their own rooms.

Mrs. Anderson had insisted on dropping each of them at their own house and watching them go in, one by one, so they hadn't had privacy to talk.

"So it's not fake," Hayley urged. "So you don't have to feel guilty."

"But it's still dishonest," said Cara.

"Maybe *technically*," said Hayley. "But I figure, look at the positive—we wouldn't have *met* her without all this. And she's a really cool girl!"

There were some things you couldn't talk about, Cara thought after she hung up. She was standing at her bedroom window, looking out over the edge of roof where she'd once encountered a small but evil thing. She thought of it now whenever she leaned out that window at night, the skate's eggs that somehow . . . hadn't been.

Some creature of the Cold, her mother had said later.

Maybe the Pouring Man could have emerged right then, if she hadn't pushed that small, ugly mass off the shingles, if it hadn't fallen. But he wouldn't bother them now. No evil things could creep toward them here anymore, now that they'd set up wards against the Cold around the neighborhood. Her mother had set the wards and strengthened them regularly, the way you'd patrol a perimeter—using the language of the old ways to protect spaces and people from the Cold and his servants. As long as the wards were up, they wouldn't be able to get in.

Last summer felt like so long ago.

Sometimes she wondered how her life would be if she'd never found out about the world beneath the world. Everything had been simpler. On the other hand, not knowing—not knowing wouldn't have been *real*. Ananda the leatherback was real, and the selkie had been real, beautiful and unknown in the dark waters. At first alarming, but then beautiful. If she hadn't found out about them she would have missed so much of what *was*.

She wouldn't have known who her own *mother* was, first of all—her strange powers, her being part of an ancient culture with its own secret knowledge. She wouldn't have known who *she* was, at least, not fully. She wouldn't have been able to bring up visions, wouldn't have believed that there were bizarre ways of moving through space that defied all she'd ever learned in science. . . .

It made her feel better about deceiving Courtney to hear how Hayley thought of it. She envied Hayley, who looked on the bright side and was practical. Hayley took things in stride. She didn't let herself get overwhelmed by the enormity of what they were facing.

Well, she could be like that too. She resolved that she *would* be. Take things in stride and keep going. What use was it to be overwhelmed, what good could it do?

Be practical. Stay focused. Act like the enormity isn't there at all.

Three

On Saturday morning their dad shut himself up in his study after breakfast to read his "peer-review documents," and the rest of the family huddled around the table over the sad remains of waffles, soggy with syrup. "The crappy part is," said Max, "that even if we win this fight, which is a huge *if*, and somehow shut down the thing with nukes, and even if we manage to stop the Cold, we'll still have global warming. I mean they drum it into our heads, Mom. We don't *need* the Cold. We're doing a stellar job of wrecking the planet without him."

Outside the big window, sun streamed down through the open spaces between the branches of a tall pine. It made a pattern on the grass that danced as the tree's dipping boughs swayed in the breeze that rose off the bay. Cara gazed at the pattern, wishing she could be suspended in sunlight and wind. Wishing what Max was saying was made up. Was that so much to ask? Maybe the scientists were wrong.

She let her vision blur as she stared, and the pattern of shadow and sun turned fuzzy.

"Well, we're on a dangerous path," said their mother after a minute, taking a sip of her coffee. "But here's the thing. We *can* change the way we live in the world. We can start repairing the harm that's been done, because we know what's happening, and we have good energy technology if we only use it. What we don't have yet is the ability to win over the powers that make those big decisions. And those powers—some of them have been working with the Cold for hundreds of years. Longer. Since the advent of coal."

"Coal's been around forever," said Jax.

"Since the Bronze Age, but it wasn't used on an Earth-changing scale till the invention of modern steam engines. Late 1700s. And what you'll never find in the history books—outside our sanctuaries, anyway—is the Cold's role in driving the technologies that use fossils. Since just before the Industrial Revolution, which he shaped, he's been promoting climate-warming technologies in every way you can think of. His allies helped develop and spread machines and economies that used fossil fuels instead of other sources and inventions—clean forms of energy like solar and wind—that would have taken us down a different road. What that means is that, if we can beat him and his powerful allies, we'll have a chance to start again."

Cara remembered something Mr. Sabin had said to her when she first went to the Institute. This must have been what he was talking about—coal, and Birmingham, England. She didn't remember the details.

Cara heard footsteps and then some toenail clicking as Puppy came bounding into the room and stood up on his hind legs to put his paws on the back of Max's chair. Their dad had come out of his office—Cara heard him moving around in the kitchen behind her, clattering dishes. "Coffee's great!" he called to their mother.

"Mom? I'll be in the backyard. If you want to talk," said Jax, scraping his chair back.

"Make sure you take your plate to the kitchen first," said their mother. "Max'll do the dishes. Won't you, Max."

Mrs. O gave Cara her next assignment a few minutes later by phone: she and Hayley needed to get into Courtney's dad's home office and copy his computer files onto a thumb drive.

"It's a special drive with a little old-ways customization on it. It'll copy all his files without needing any password authority—and it'll do it very, very fast. All you need to do is stick it in his computer's USB port, count to twenty and pull it out again. The computer doesn't even have to be on. It's in the glove compartment of your mother's car in the back of a hairbrush. It's got a panel. You'll see."

James Bond, thought Cara as she trudged outside toward the car parked in the driveway. *And here, 007, you have an ingenious spy hairbrush.* At least now she had the chance to do something concrete. She was glad.

Sprinklers were going back and forth on one of her neighbors' lawns, and tall pink hollyhocks swayed over the top of a wooden fence. Her mother didn't bother to lock her old, shabby car when it was parked at home, so Cara popped the door open and was leaning into the passenger side, with the glove box gaping, when someone slapped the seat of her jeans. Hard.

She jumped up, squealing.

"Gotcha," said Hayley.

"Hilarious," said Cara, and leaned back into the car to feel around in the glove compartment and pull out a tortoiseshell hairbrush. "*So* funny."

When she righted herself she saw Courtney walking across the yard behind Hay.

"Courtney!" she said, and instinctively stuck the hairbrush behind her back. Then she remembered it was a *hairbrush*. And told herself to relax.

Courtney was spinning a yo-yo and catching it in a way that looked accomplished; Cara hadn't known anyone even played with yo-yos anymore.

"I rode along with my mom," said Courtney. "I wanted to pick up a couple things at the market for us to snack on during the marathon."

"Marathon?" asked Cara.

"I didn't have time to tell you, Car, we're watching more of Season One today," said Hayley. "You into it?"

So the James Bond mission could be carried out today, Cara thought. But would she have a chance to clue Hayley in? Or would she have to do it all by herself?

"Sure, OK," she said. "I just have to check with my parents."

"I thought we could maybe go swimming after," said Courtney. "If you're into swimming on the bayside. The water's kind of nasty with all the seaweed and other gunk."

"Tell us about it. We've swum in that backwash all our lives," said Hayley.

"I'll get my stuff," said Cara.

⚎

Jax had to push, his mother said. That was what she'd started calling it when he dove his mind into the Internet and went flying through the volumes. Cub wouldn't get far without him. They were standing in the backyard near where the ground began sloping down to the water, in the patchy shade of the pines. No one else was nearby, and the air was still: other than their own voices, all he could hear was the faint lap of the waves.

He, not Cub, was the key to breaking into the Chinese supercomputer, she said. That part was down to him. Cub just had to leave some lines of code once they got there.

"Sometimes I wish I was still allowed to ping," he said suddenly. "You guys, I mean. It'd be easier to—"

"Only in a crisis, Jax. Come on. You know the dangers," said his mom.

"I guess," he said. But it was true: what he gained in factual knowledge never made up for the shame he felt when he infringed on someone else's thoughts. Because stealth-pinging was a form of injury, not only to the

68

person whose mind was being invaded but also to the one doing it.

Minds were messy places, where beasts could rear up at you suddenly or you could step on stray rusty nails. Inside the minds of his friends and family there were pictures of him that looked like reflections in funhouse mirrors. And the worst part of it was that those funhouse mirror images weren't even distorted on *purpose*. Cara had always loved him and stood up for him, for example, but in her mind his image was little and cute and at the same time overlaid with stereotyped ideas about Einstein and Tesla and genius. When he ran into those mental pictures they made him feel distant from her. It hurt because he didn't *want* to be apart from her. She was his closest ally in the world.

And Max's mind—well, in Max's mind he'd mostly been an irritation, when he used to ping there. To Max he'd been like a mouse that squeaks around your feet as you're walking, making you trip and biting your toes—a mouse you're tempted to step on.

At least, that was how it used to be. He didn't stealth-ping any of them anymore, so these days he didn't know how they saw him. He hoped it was in a better light than it used to be.

Out in the bay, he heard the sound of a powerboat grow louder, then fade away again.

"Push from the beginning. Push toward your idea of Tianhe-2. Even though you don't know anything about it *technically.* Maybe do a little research first, look up where it is physically, geographically, at the university in Guangzhou. Hold in your mind where Guangzhou is in relation to where *we* are. You never know what might give you a vector that helps get you there."

So much of what Jax did was about gestures he didn't even understand *himself*—intuitions that were completely simple and ridiculously complicated at the same time. His old-ways talents felt natural but were impossible to break down into parts, like the moment when you first learned to ride a bike, the first freedom of balancing. That was what his abilities felt like to him: basic instincts he had no hope of explaining. You either knew them or you didn't. You had them or you never would.

It wasn't something he was proud of either. The same way it was with bike riding, each new talent, once he had a handle on it, turned into something he *always* should have been able to do—knowledge that had somehow been rediscovered.

"What is it Cub's inputting, if I do get us in?" he asked. "You haven't told us yet."

"Actually," said his mom. "I told *him*. We spoke."

"But it's not secret from me, is it?"

"Essentially it'll seem to be coming from inside the Chinese intelligence services and will tip them off about the admiral's plans, making clear he's a criminal and a renegade. And it'll highlight the dangers of communicating this information to anyone outside the Oval Office. Beijing has the leverage to get to the president. If you and Cub

succeed, the source will look impeccable and the Chinese
will act."

"Um . . . it seems kind of far-fetched. And risky. Doesn't
it?"

"Of all the powerhouse nations, we think the Chinese
will use the intelligence most discreetly. We don't believe
the world can handle knowledge of the Cold yet, so right
now we need this nuclear escapade shut down *without*
exposure of the carbon war and the story behind it. Some
of our friends in Shanghai and Tianjin brought us an
opportunity."

Her phone rang in her pants pocket and she fished it
out, checked it.

"Hayley's mom. I better take it," she said.

So Jax had left her on her cell—probably reassuring Mrs. M that Hayley wasn't up to any mischief—and
trudged around to the front yard just in time to see Cara
being driven off in a white car with gold trim. It had to be
the admiral's wife; they didn't know anyone else who drove
a car like that.

Then he sat on the curb, listening to a podcast about the
Chinese supercomputer complex and waiting. Cub had told
his parents he needed a ride to a library in Chatham to use
some online reference system they had for his SETI project;
he'd said that Jax, also eager to locate stray extraterrestrials,
had begged to go with him.

Jax threw pebbles at the ground as he waited, daring
them to bounce up and hit his legs. He resented Cub's

parents. Didn't they know he was Cub's only friend? How could it possibly be better for Cub to be separated from him?

He hoped he wouldn't have to talk to them.

When their car pulled up, Cub's dad was at the wheel and his mother was in the passenger seat, typing on a tablet, as usual. Well, he'd keep his eyes on his phone. Maybe he'd even keep his earbuds in. That was the rudest he could be.

Of course, knowing Cub's parents they wouldn't even notice.

At Courtney's house Cara asked for a tour, so she'd know where she was supposed to be snooping. Her beach bag hung off her shoulder, the bristles on the spy hairbrush poking into her side.

"This is the workout room," said Courtney as they passed it. "My mom's Pilates machine and my dad's punching bag. Sometimes I think they should switch. My mom's the one who needs a punching bag and my dad could stand to improve his flexibility . . . you know? And this room's a home sauna. Except I can't stand saunas. They make me feel like I can't breathe."

Cara was barely listening to them. She felt so nervous, she couldn't have a casual conversation.

"So is your dad home?" asked Hayley.

"Nah," said Courtney. "He's off on an aircraft carrier somewhere. Training exercises or whatever. He's Sixth Fleet, so he's hardly ever around."

"Is that, like, the Army?" said Hay.

"The Navy," said Courtney, grinning. "They're the ones with the ships. You really know your armed forces!"

"Yeah, I'm super-military," said Hayley. "Totes warlike and ultraviolent. That's me."

"That's his office," said Courtney as they passed a closed door. "This is the laundry room, big thrill. . . ."

After they settled down to watch the show, Cara waited as long as she could stand to, nervousness mounting. She wondered what excuse she could use to leave the room—Courtney had her own bathroom, right off the bedroom, so *that* excuse was out.

"Courtney," came her mom's voice from the hallway, right on cue. "I'm going out to run an errand. You girls OK here for half an hour?"

"Yeah, Mom," said Courtney, robotically.

"Let's swim," said Hayley suddenly. "I'm feeling kinda beachy."

This was Cara's chance. She changed into her suit and some cutoff shorts in the bathroom—Hayley was wearing hers underneath—and fiddled with the hairbrush until the back popped off. Sure enough, there was a small compartment, like the ones used for batteries, and inside was a thumb drive.

It didn't *look* special.

She shoved it in the pocket of the jeans shorts, and when she emerged from Courtney's bathroom again she said she had a stomachache.

Would the others mind if she just stayed in the house, maybe lay down and waited for them?

"Hey, we don't *have* to go," said Courtney. "You want us to hang with you and see if it gets better?"

"No, go, it's really fine," said Cara, feeling a pang over how nice Courtney was being. "I'll just play a game on my phone and wait to feel better. It's no big deal."

She listened to the two of them clomp down the stairs, Hayley in heavy clogs, Courtney in flips; then she turned and watched through Courtney's bedroom window as they disappeared down the staircase at the cliff's edge. They became visible again picking their way across the beach away from her, colorful, striped beach towels slung over their shoulders. Once they got in the water, she figured, she had at least five minutes before they could make it back to the house, even if they hated the water and came right out again. And Courtney's mother had driven off on her errand. Cara turned away from the window and went out of the bedroom and down the hall to the office door. Her heart sped up as she turned the knob.

But it was locked.

And now she saw a number pad on the wall beside the door. You had to have a *code* to get into the admiral's study.

Mrs. O must not have known that, she thought, and for a second she felt like she was dangling, all by herself, over a chasm.

She had the easiest job of anyone. And she was already failing at it.

She went to the next door along and opened it instead: Courtney's parents' bedroom. Courtney hadn't showed them that room, either, on the tour—it had a huge four-poster bed with a carved wooden headboard and draperies hanging from it. It seemed vaguely royal, Cara thought—the way she imagined the beds of ancient queens and kings. Cut flowers stood in vases, and old-fashioned paintings of proud-looking people lined one wall. There was a door onto a long bathroom with two sinks, side by side, where perfume bottles sparkled on glass shelves; and last but not least, there was a big, wrap-around balcony outside the sliding glass doors, overlooking the ocean.

She slid the glass door open and stepped out. The Andersons' house, unlike her family's, was on a headland jutting out at the edge of the cove. The sound of the waves was louder on this hilltop: they were exposed up here, not tucked into marsh and woods.

There in the shallows were Hayley and Courtney, standing and trailing their arms back and forth. They were facing outward so that Cara could see only the backs of their heads—and farther out a small sailboat passed, its pale-yellow sail flapping in the breeze.

She followed the balcony as it wrapped around the house, and sure enough, there were sliding doors into the next room over too. Which had to be Mr. Anderson's office. (Admiral Anderson? Did you call admirals mister?) She couldn't see into the room because it was hidden by long blinds. For sure these doors would be locked too, she thought, but reached out to check the handle.

Yep. Locked.

Now her heart really sank. *Fail.*

The girls' voices carried to her over the water—*Cara! Cara! Hey, Cara!* She turned and waved. They were wading out of the water, splashing the water in front of them . . . so they'd seen her. She walked along the balcony, pretending a casual stroll while taking in the view. How to get into that office?

Would *Courtney* know the code?

She turned a corner as the balcony wrapped around to the side of the house; steps led down to the yard, where she stood and watched as Hay and Courtney came up the beach path. Their hair and swimsuited bodies were dripping as they laughed about something.

And then, as she stood waiting, it occurred to her: What if she'd left the parents' bedroom door open?

She couldn't remember. Maybe she had.

She crossed her arms and gripped them with her fingers, hard.

But when she got there, Courtney didn't ask what she'd been doing on the balcony, only how her stomach was. (Her thoughtfulness made Cara feel even guiltier.) And when they trooped upstairs again, the parents' bedroom door *was* closed—she'd done one thing right, at least.

"Hey! We have to get into her dad's study," she hissed at Hay while Courtney was in the bathroom, changing out of her suit. "It's locked. There's a code. But I have to get in!"

"Who're these guys?" asked Hayley a few minutes later. The three of them were headed downstairs to forage for snack foods, but Hayley had stopped in front of some pictures in the upstairs hallway, pretending to be interested in an old black-and-white shot of a bunch of guys in white uniforms and hats that bore the legend *United States Naval Academy. 1950.*

"That's when my grandfather graduated from Annapolis, I guess," said Courtney. "It's kind of a family tradition. . . ."

"So, like, what do guys in the Navy do?" asked Hayley.

"What do they *do*! When they're not fighting in wars, you mean?"

"I didn't even know they used that many ships in wars anymore," said Hayley. "Isn't it mostly planes and tanks? Color me clueless."

"They use ships to move planes around, for one thing. Sometimes my dad's on carriers, which are, like, huge concrete boats that feel like small cities," said Courtney.

"Does he keep like guns at home, or whatever?" said Hayley. "If he does, just don't tell my mom, OK? She won't let me come over. She's super-paranoid about weapons."

"I don't know," said Courtney, surprised by the question. "They'd be locked up if he did, for sure. See, the thing is, I've never spent that much time around my parents. The only reason I am *now* is, they lost a bunch of money and had to downsize everything. The money's from my mom's side, actually. My dad keeps saying how temporary this is. I guess they must be bummed to actually have to *live* with me, right?"

"Get out," said Hayley.

"Of *course* not," said Cara. "That's probably the silver lining for them."

"You guys are optimists," said Courtney. "I mean, I guess my mom likes me OK. But my dad—he was the one who made her send me off to school in the first place."

In the kitchen—as Courtney opened cabinets rapid-fire and asked *Chips? Pretzels? Cheese puffs?*—Hayley shot a sidelong look at Cara, like "I'm trying." Or that was what Cara *thought* it meant. Cara should help her, she knew, but she couldn't think of a single natural-sounding thing to ask Courtney that would lead them into the admiral's study.

"Is your dad a fox?" said Hayley suddenly.

Courtney was bent over looking for drinks in the bottom of the fridge. She straightened and turned around, looking incredulous.

"Are you *kidding*?"

"What? They say guys in uniform are hot, don't they?" asked Hayley wide-eyed, like it was a normal and innocent question. "Cara was just giving me a hard time about liking Marc Anthony. I can't think guys in their fifties are eye candy?"

"Gross, Hay," said Cara. "Dis*gus*ting."

But she could tell Hayley was on a path of conversation aimed at trying to get them into that locked office.

"Way gross. My dad is *not* handsome," said Courtney. "I've seen snaggletooth bulldogs that are cuter than him."

"Prove it," said Hayley. "I bet you just don't see it because he's your father. I bet he's a stone fox in his whole white-hat-with-the-black-visor-deal."

And unbelievably, it worked. A couple of seconds later, shaking her head ruefully, Courtney had abandoned their snacks on the counter, a pile of chips bags and cracker boxes, and was taking the stairs two at a time ahead of them. At her dad's door, she punched in a code—though Cara wasn't at the right angle to see it. So it would have to be *now*, she thought, and felt in her shorts pocket for the thumb drive.

Still there.

The door clicked, and they followed Courtney in.

"I rest my case," she said and turned, raising her hand like she was presenting a prize: a wall of photos.

It was a bunch of men in suits, Cara saw, her eyes skipping away from the pictures to the desk and computer. Important-looking old men standing beside the same guy in a white uniform with lots of medals on his chest and dignified-looking epaulets—a man who, it was true, was red-faced, balding, and yeah: probably not as good-looking as a bulldog with bad teeth.

"Hmm," said Hayley, pausing in front of the wall and pretending to deliberate. She and Courtney both stood looking at it, with Cara hovering behind them—*Now?* she thought. *Now?*

She stepped back a few steps, away from the other two and toward the desk, her hand in her pocket, fingers on the thumb drive. The computer, a desktop with a big monitor, was a kind of PC she didn't recognize. Where would the ports be?

"Well, so . . . ," said Hayley, delaying painfully.

"Admit it," said Courtney.

"OK. You were right. I was wrong. Your dad is *not* foxy."

She and Courtney both burst out laughing.

"Wait," said Hayley, and Cara knew she was playing for time again. She leaned forward and felt around the back of the unit with her fingers, then along one side . . . but no ports yet. "Are those all, like, famous dudes he's in the photos with? Who's *that*?"

"Uh . . . you mean Ronald Reagan?" said Courtney.

Finally. She felt what should be the right shape of hole. She slipped the thumb drive out of her pocket, praying that Courtney didn't pick now to turn around.

"And this guy?"

"George H. W. Bush . . . Hayley, are you pulling my leg? You don't recognize their faces? These guys were, like, the *presidents*."

There. Cara stuck the thumb drive in the port and snatched back her hand—just as Courtney turned around and looked at her. She froze for a second, pulse racing. Then decided to act normal. She reached for a photo beside the monitor on the desk, picked it up and looked at it.

It was another picture of himself. In uniform again—but this one when he was young. The guy had to be totally selfish.

"Hayley's proud to be ignorant. Hayley's the *hoi polloi*," she said, keeping her voice casual as she pretended to be interested in the picture.

"Completely *hoi*," agreed Hayley. "But I know that one on the left. Bill Clinton."

"What, do you think *he's* a fox too?" asked Courtney.

It must have been twenty seconds now. Or maybe not. Could she hold out five more seconds? One, two, three, four—she snaked her hand forward and unplugged the thumb drive from the port.

Stuffed it back into her pocket.

"*Now* who's kidding who," said Hayley. "Come on. He's totally Jurassic! Grandfather age. Plus he looks like a friendly hamster."

"Your bff is a weirdo," said Courtney to Cara, shaking her head. "Come on. Let's get out of here before my mom comes home."

⊰⊱

"That was out of *control*," said Cub. "I wasn't ready. And then the librarian was standing over me—I think she was worried you were having a seizure—"

They were in the bathroom in the library, both feeling shaky. It was the kind of "family" public restroom where you could lock the door and have it to yourself, and it smelled of diapers. A grimy plastic changing table that folded down from the wall had a picture of a koala bear on it.

But at least it was private.

"Sorry," said Jax, trying to steady his breathing. "I didn't know I'd—I mean I didn't know how it would be. I didn't know I'd look any different from normal."

"Good thing she was apparently blind as a bat," said Cub. "Or maybe the CIA would be here. Man."

Jax had been sitting beside Cub, both of them at the same computer this time, pushing as Cub clicked from page to page. He'd watched avidly as pages came up that said Cub needed registrations or security clearance or passwords or usernames or whatever else, and whenever one of those restricted-access warnings came up, he pushed through it. He filed back to the materials he'd read on the Tianhe 2 and then he just pushed toward it, and one by one the pages disappeared and time after time they were in.

Jax didn't even know *what* they were in, only that they were breaking through a maze of firewalls as they crossed the virtual fields.

Cub's mouth had hung open—whenever Jax pushed past a privacy barrier, he couldn't believe it. He kept typing anyway, in a state of keyed-up amazement, his fingers flying over the keyboard faster than Jax could ever have typed.

But the more Jax pushed the more the library around him receded. Cub faded away beside him, the hard wooden chair he was sitting on turned soft beneath him, and everything in the real world sank into a blurry haze with a soundtrack that was like a soup on a low boil: it made almost no noise and then there'd be a gurgle of sound like a bubble popping on the surface. It was mind noise, Jax knew: his guard went down as he focused on pushing, and now and then he pinged by accident, as he hunkered there on the chair he hardly felt anymore—he pinged a bystander at random and heard something burst out of their mind like a bubble in soup.

Once it was Cub, because the ping said some stuff about coding he didn't get, and once it must have been the librarian, who was the only other person in the room. *Got to talk to that Acquisitions guy about the missing—*

Other than the bubbles popping there was nothing, it was like a sinkhole, where all he saw was the depth of the data screen, the seemingly infinite universe of digits in there, so deep it was overwhelming. He spun and spun, delving, and it was like flying through piles of things—maybe metal things, except that they didn't cut him but seemed to flap at him as he went, faster and faster. Then it turned a corner and felt bad and dangerous. The edges were sharper, and dark lines crept toward him whose meaning he couldn't comprehend. The lines were like finger bones, somehow, or the triangle teeth of bear traps—he didn't know why, but he knew it suddenly wasn't safe.

He was being handled. Someone was shaking him.

"Hey! Are you OK? Can you tell me your name?"

His eyes were terribly sore. They ached. The librarian had turned his chair away from the monitor and had her hands on his shoulders.

"Yeah, uh—"

"Rodney!" burst out Cub.

"I needed *him* to tell me," scolded the librarian, and then her face was near Jax's again. "Do you know where you are, Rodney?"

"Uh. Puh—public library," said Jax.

"You weren't blinking! Look how red his eyes are! There were tears running down your face, honey. I was afraid you weren't breathing or something, your face was so stiff—and then the eyes—"

"He's fine," said Cub. "He gets like this. He's just a spaz. You're fine now, aren't you, Rodney?"

That had been the name on the fake library card, a super-stiff name that sounded as fake as it was. Rodney Harford. But it was a good thing Cub had spoken up, because he'd been so out of it himself that he might easily have said his real name.

"'He's a spaz'?" asked Jax. "That was your attempt at a medical explanation for how I was acting?"

In the small bathroom, Cub was pacing back and forth.

"You didn't blink, man. I don't think you blinked for *minutes*. Look at your eyes!"

Jax turned to the mirror—his eyes were so bloodshot they looked practically solid red where the whites should be. And the skin of his face was white. He did look unhealthy.

"Huh," he said. "No wonder she thought something was wrong with me."

"Point is," said Cub, "we made it *in*, Jax. Incredible. We made it *in*!"

"We did?"

Jax had almost no memory of what had gone down at the end of the push. He recalled being surrounded by this heavy, dense data that felt like a million tons of—he didn't know. Tanks. Lead. Razor blades. In those last instants where the real world had become blurry, the virtual world had become sharp all over, its edges spiking around him, black, branching cracks that spidered toward him—

"But I didn't get done," said Cub, and shook his head. "We have to go back again. I didn't get finished. I had to exit in a hurry when she came running over."

"Oh," said Jax, nodding. He felt the energy drain out of him. "So we have to go back in. . . ."

"Man, I don't know how you *did* it," said Cub, "but you could make millions as a hacker. *Hundreds* of millions. I mean you could get into anything. You could steal, like, all of the world's money."

"Uh, that's OK," said Jax.

But he felt terribly weak. He didn't want to face Cub's annoying parents for the ride home.

His legs went rubbery, and he sat down abruptly on the bathroom floor.

"Jax!" said Cub. "Hey! Hacker king! You *are* OK, aren't you?"

Cub sounded increasingly scared. Jax wondered why, but was too drained to pursue the thought.

"I'm really tired," he said in a small voice.

He wanted his mother. His father. Cara or Max, even.

"Um—shoot—I'm going to call your mom, actually. Not my parents—they won't know what to—"

Jax closed his eyes, finally, and rested the back of his head on the smooth tiled wall. He knew it felt nice and cool. And then he didn't know anything.

"You did it!" said Hayley.

"I guess so," said Cara doubtfully. "If we *got* anything. I guess we'll find out when I hand the thumb drive over to mom."

She and Hayley were at Hayley's house; when they got back they'd been locked out and the spare key wasn't in the usual spot. Her father had gone to his office in Barnstable, she knew, but she didn't know where her mother was, or her brothers, and her phone had run out of juice.

And Hayley's mom was working at the salon, but Mrs. Anderson hadn't known that when she dropped them off.

"Can you text Max?" she asked Hayley. "He checks his phone way more than my mom checks hers. And Jax was working with Cub. I don't want to bug them. Just tell Max to pick me up here on his way home?"

As Hayley texted busily Cara cruised along her kitchen counter, keeping an idle lookout for snacks. Mrs. M sometimes baked—especially the premade cookies from plastic tubes, which Cara actually liked better than cookies made from scratch. Disappointing: no cookies in the glass jar . . . but next to the jar, sticking out from under the edge of a *People* magazine, she saw a headline: NEANDERTHALS AND HUMANS CO-EXISTED LONGER THAN PREVIOUSLY THOUGHT.

She moved the *People* aside, curious. It was a stapled printout from some other magazine, spotted with drops of spilled coffee.

"How come your mom's reading *this*?" she asked Hayley.

"Huh?" asked Hayley. She finished up her texting and peered over Cara's shoulder as she passed. "I dunno. Maybe the Neanderthals had little-known beauty tips. Did you see any chocolate chips around? No? That really sucks."

Cara scanned the beginning of the article.

Neanderthals were long believed by archaeologists to have died out about 500 years after modern humans first arrived. New research reveals the two species likely lived alongside each other in Europe for up to 5,000 years — and even interbred.

"It's so weird she'd be reading this," she murmured, but Hayley was already headed up the short flight of stairs to her bedroom.

"I think we can set aside the idea of a rapid extinction of Neanderthals caused solely by the arrival of

modern humans. Instead we can see a more complex
process in which there is a much longer overlap and
could have been exchanges of ideas and culture," says
lead researcher Professor Thomas Higham of Oxford
University.

"He already texted back!" yelled Hayley from upstairs.
"What?"
"Max! He said something's up. He said to meet in the castle."

Hayley's backyard, unlike the Sykeses', didn't border the water of the bay but a wooded area. Through the woods you could see an old tree house that had once belonged to some other neighborhood kids, long since grown up and moved away.

Back when they were little, Cara and Hayley had sat there for whole afternoons; they'd kept snacks in a cubby there and in another cubby a box of books (for Cara) and Barbies (for Hayley). They'd fitted it out with an old rug on the floor and a tarp that hung overhead to give them shade, because the roof was missing. The wood of the tree house was painted white, though most of the paint had blistered off, and in places you could still see the faint rounded outlines of gray, painted-on stones. The stones had already been faded when they first discovered the place, but they'd always called it "the castle."

It was always a risk to go to the castle, because the path was thick with poison ivy. But if you knew where to step, you'd be fine—and adults were sure to leave you alone. They shouted new warnings about the poison ivy every time they saw you heading out, but they never followed you.

"I haven't been here in years," said Cara as they picked their way along the path, over a carpet of old mulch and soil. The serrated ivy leaves trembled as the girls clomped along the narrow path, which was damp and sprouted clusters of yellow mushrooms they crushed underfoot. "Have you?"

"Not since the last time we came here together, probably," said Hayley. "What were we, nine or ten?"

Cara flashed back to a buggy evening in summer when they'd been out in the castle at dusk and suddenly it had started pouring, water pooling on top of the tarp and making it sag lower and lower as thunder boomed close around them. That was the only time an adult had ventured into the castle: Hayley's mom, who showed up with her hair in crazy-looking foils, carrying an umbrella roughly the size of a VW Beetle. She'd ushered them back to the house in a panic, convinced they were going to be struck by lightning.

Max was already there, typing on his phone as they came up.

"Wait, wait," he said, and finished his texting. "OK. Something's happened."

"Where's mom?" asked Cara.

"She's with Jax. Listen. We got a tip that maybe there's an attack coming, that the wards around the neighborhood are at risk tonight. The western ward lines are already down, the ones at the waterline. So we have to get out."

"But—but they've been fine for *months*," said Cara. "Since—so why—all of a sudden—"

"Because of what else is going on," Max said. "Mom said the Cold must have decided we need to be, uh, *neutralized*. Before the bomb deploys. Or Jax does, anyway. Since, as we all know, it's only Jax that matters."

"Jealous much?" said Hayley.

"They're sending someone. Or some*thing*," said Max, ignoring her. "Mom needs us to hunker down in a ward stronghold while she deals with it."

"A ward stronghold? What's that?" asked Hayley.

"In this case," said Max, "it's the Institute. It was re-warded after that Burner invasion, so it's super-fortified now. I'm supposed to drive you guys there. Mom even warded her car—it's parked over on Spruce. We aren't sup-posed to go to the house again, just in case."

"But my mom—what should I tell *her*?" asked Hayley.

"It's squared away already. Sleepover in a friend's beach house in Chatham, is the story. So Cara can help you study for your last exam. Mrs. M's cool with it. Come on."

He led them through the woods, perpendicular to their own street on a path that ran beneath the trees behind strangers' backyard fences. She was so focused on avoiding the telltale serrated leaves looming close to her feet—and then on watching for neighbors who might yell at them for trespassing—that she barely looked up until they finally zigzagged across an unfenced backyard with a jungle gym in it.

When they emerged from between two houses onto the street, there was their mother's car.

And there, in the front passenger seat, sat Zee.

Cara froze in her tracks. Max, ahead of her and Hayley, kept walking.

From behind the windshield, Zee raised her face and looked at Cara. Was she smiling?

"Max! What *is* this?" Cara called out to his back, alarmed.

"Just come on," he said without turning.

"But she's—didn't we think the bad guys could *get* to us through her?" hissed Hayley, stopped on the sidewalk beside Cara. "I thought that's what we decided, I thought she "

"We're not supposed to go *near* her," said Cara. "It was *agreed.*"

"I couldn't just leave her," said Max, turning to them with his hand on the door handle. "It's not her fault. Anything could happen to her. It's not right."

He opened the door.

"But Max, did Mom say it was—"

"Come on," he said. "We've got to go. We're sitting ducks!"

And he got in.

Paralyzed, the girls looked at each other.

"Is it even safe to get in the car with her?" asked Hayley.

"It's not safe out *here* either," said Cara. "You heard him. And if the car's warded, the Cold can't make his creatures come through her while she's inside it. Can he?"

"How should *I* know? Those rules are all Greek to me."

She leaned in close to Cara's ear.

"She creeps me *out*," she whispered. "Even when she smiles—see? Look how she *smiles*."

Cara followed her gaze. It was true, Zee's smile did look a bit frozen. Like a doll's.

But she might just be nervous.

After another minute of Max sitting behind the steering wheel and glaring out at them with his door ajar, and twice yelling "Come on! Now!" Cara finally walked to the car, Hayley trailing. They got into the back, slamming the doors behind them, and Cara heard a click-click from the doors as Max hit the button that locked them all in.

"Hi, guys," said Zee from the front seat, sounding more hesitant than Cara remembered. She turned around and smiled briefly.

She seemed pretty normal. But then, if you were a vessel or a hollow, you wouldn't necessarily know it.

Cara had never *seen* Zee up close since she found out she was probably working with the Cold. Max had said he'd seen her in the house where the terrible old lady attacked her—that it *was* Zee Cara'd caught sight of in the distance on the oil-drilling rig with the black eyes of a hollow—but they'd never known for sure. And Zee's eyes weren't black now; they were their usual color, a pale gray.

Cara had always liked Zee for her laid-back attitude, her friendly and open manner. And she'd felt sorry for her, too, since Max had to dump her. It wasn't fair. Zee had been, for *years* before they started going out, his best friend.

"Hi," said Cara, and then didn't know what else to say.

"Hi," added Hayley dutifully.

How much did Zee know?

"She's coming with us to the safe house," said Max.

"Did you, uh, tell her what's . . . going on?" asked Cara.

That was general enough, she figured. It wouldn't give anything away, in case Zee was still in the dark.

"I asked her to trust me. You trust me, right, Zee?"

"I trust you," said Zee obediently.

There was something different about her, Cara was sure. She was less confident, less sharp than the old Zee. She almost had . . . less *personality*. But was she just acting different because of the breakup, because she and Max weren't close anymore?

Cara wondered if she was always like this now—less sure of herself, shyer. Not as happy.

"Hey, Max," she said, pulling her phone from the pocket of her windbreaker, "can you plug in my phone up there? The battery's drained."

Max was leaning forward to plug it in when the windshield smashed into a thousand pieces.

Zee screamed, throwing herself backward so hard that her seat crashed against Cara's knees and sent her back too. A furry blackness was beating and scrabbling across the whole windshield, covering the glass—no, not furry, *feathery*. A volley of thuds had cracked the window from one side to another, but still the sheet of glass hadn't fallen in: it was a web of cracks. Smears of blood were being wiped into a mist by splayed blue-black feathers and scrabbling gray claws.

It wasn't one bird—it was many. They were crows or maybe ravens, she didn't know the difference, but they were large and black. Were they angry?

"You said it was warded!" yelled Hayley.

"They're just birds," shouted Max over the sound of Zee's shrieks. "They're *birds*!"

The crows writhed and flapped on the glass, blocking all the light, smearing their injured wings and croaking out terrible caws—loud, raw sounds that made Cara want to plug her ears. What were they doing? She desperately wanted to jump out of the car—had the wards really *failed*? *Already?*—and reached out to grab her door handle.

"No!" said Max. "Cara. Stay! Don't get out—it's not them, the crows are *not* the threat! Something *scared* them!"

Her hand still on the door handle, Cara watched as the birds kept writhing. Their movements gradually slowed, though a few talons still scratched here and there, pulling loose pebbles of glass with them so that the windshield began to sag inward. Finally the dreadful croaks trailed off into silence. Some of the birds flipped and struggled still against the wreckage; one dragged a broken wing as it fell off the side of the car's hood, hitting Zee's side-view mirror as it went.

Others slid down slowly, hard to see in any detail through the broken glass.

"It's safety glass, it may not fall out of the frame yet," said Max, shaking his head, "but I can't *drive* like this. I can't see anything."

"But we have to get out of here!" said Hayley. "Bird blood! And—"

"The birds are just birds," said Max. "That's why the wards didn't stop them, but whatever scared them—it has to be nearby, doesn't it?"

"Knock out the windshield!" said Hayley. "We *have* to. Better to have just a busted-out window in a car that's mostly protected than have to get out of the car and run for it when there's something dangerous right here—and no wards at all! Where would we run to anyway? Nowhere's safe but the Institute—right, Max?"

"What *is* this?" asked Zee, her voice high. "What's *happening?*"

"I'll do it," said Max, "I'll get out and—"

"Wait," said Cara. "Shh, please be quiet, guys. Just give me a minute of quiet. *Please!*" Adrenalin was rushing through her; right now she thought she *could* do what she needed to. She thought she could ask to see. She would do it—she *would.*

She closed her eyes and thought of a wash of water falling down, she thought fast and hard of a rush of water that fell like a sheet of sameness and blocked out everything else, even the sounds of the few bird claws still scrabbling on the metal. No claws. No sounds. Water. Water, water, a wall of it. It helped to clear her mind.

Then she held the birds in her thoughts, opened her feelings as wide as she could, and asked.

And in her mind's eye she was outside the car, seeing the broken bodies of the ravens on the shattered, nearly opaque windshield, a pile of dead ones heaped over the dormant wipers, where they'd slid down the glass. She felt a pang for them.

Then she was flying up and away—lifting off street level, floating up into the trees, spinning in the air over houses and telephone poles. She was moving along the wires between the poles, zooming along the cable, then over the metal at the top of the pole and along the droop of the wire again. She swooped along and down the next pole and into a fenced-in area where there were machines—some kind of fenced-in area for electrical equipment, she thought, with orange signs on the chain-link that warned of high voltage.

The earth. Something in the soil moved, a hump in the ground, slithering and disappearing beneath the earth and then showing itself again. Something pink-brown, something that gleamed wetly, showed its skin through the dirt that fell aside. Looking at it she felt as if her own skin was shrinking on her bones, felt an ugly creeping fear, and then she looked up again and saw something else. It flew down, blotting out the sun.

When it touched the ground, in a blur and a cloud of dust, it changed—now it was a tall, four-legged animal, something like an anteater or a camel or a cross between them, big, hairy, and tan-colored. It crouched and snuffled, stamped the soil with its great, shaggy hooves. She knew it was an animal that wasn't alive anymore—she thought maybe she'd seen its picture once in some book of extinct animals. Yes. It looked like an animal that had disappeared a long time ago.

That meant it had to be Q, Q in a different form, because Q, her mom had said, was more ancient than the rest of them and could mimic those ancient forms . . . she wished Jax were here—maybe he could even ping it, read its mind and tell her if it was on their side—

It shook the ground where the slithering thing moved, stamped and lowered its head. But then the slimy thing was lunging at it, and she saw it had sharp parts, like curved fangs or pincers, that tore at the creature's legs and feet as it reared up and back. They tore at the camel-creature's legs and it was horrible—she could see bone on one of them. But Q kept coming, kept bearing down on it with kicking feet, and gradually it was stomped down into the soil . . . the fanged thing shrank down, down, down.

After a few seconds the dirt settled behind it and was still.

Then Q swung its head up from the ground and morphed again, its torn and bloody legs disappearing into its body as it sprouted outrageous wings and shifted into another form. But it staggered as it did this, and Cara could swear it was in pain.

Still it rose into the air again and was away—and Cara was just sitting in the car again, vision passed, staring at the smashed windshield with its smears and pile of black bodies.

They were safe. For now. For now, Q had gotten rid of the threat for them.

"OK," she said, and jumped out of the car. "Guys! Help me!"

They found sticks and pried off the lacy remains of the windshield, peeling it off in sections so that it collapsed along its fault lines onto the hood of the car. Hayley held a rolled-up newspaper and helped sweep the pieces off the dash. It was frustrating—they had to get as much of it as they could because otherwise the pieces would blow back on them as they drove. Zee stayed in the car, not helping but just staring out at them from between the edges of the ragged hole in the glass; when Cara caught sight of her she looked a little none-too-bright with her slack-jawed expression.

"We're OK for the moment," she told Max and Hayley breathlessly, trying not to look at the heads of the dead ravens as she swept one onto the pavement. The heads were the worst by far—the open black eyes, smart and still wet with life, the beaks that were cracked open to show pink tongues. "Q scared it away, I'm pretty sure. I don't know what the birds saw exactly—or sensed—it was sticking out of the ground—some creature of the Cold's. But either it'll come back or something else will. So we have to move fast."

Hayley shrieked, and Cara felt her body tense up. But it was just a raven: one of the broken creatures was still alive—barely. It fluttered against Hayley's newspaper and then fell limply onto the grass beside the sidewalk.

Then they were sitting in the car again, slamming the doors, and Max started it up. The faster they went, the harder the wind whipped over the hood and into their faces. Bits of leftover glass were still lodged in cracks in the seats up front and on the carpet, and Cara, tears streaming from her eyes whenever she tried to face forward, searched frantically in the door compartments and seatback pouches for anything she could hold over her face to block the fast-moving air. Hayley, at least, had the newspaper she'd been sweeping with, but Cara couldn't find anything else to block the wind.

Plus, as soon as they got onto the fast part of Route 6 past the Orleans roundabout, bugs were flying at them with the high-speed onrush of air too. Still, Cara and Hayley were lucky to be in the backseat, where, if they positioned their faces directly behind the headrests, they didn't get the worst of it.

Zee stayed hunkered down in the front so that her face was out of the wind and protected from bugs by the dashboard—but Max, at the steering wheel, had to sit up straight to have a clear view. He'd borrowed Cara's sunglasses, and Hayley, sitting behind him, took a bandanna she found wadded up on the floor and—with some difficulty and a few swearwords from Max—leaned forward and tied it around his nose and mouth.

They didn't have time to pull over, because the longer they took to get where they were going, the more danger they were putting themselves in. There was no shoulder on this part of the road anyway.

"This thing *stinks*," complained Max, muffled, through the cotton fabric.

"Oh yeah," said Cara, remembering. "That's the cloth I used to wipe up Puppy's drool that time he slobbered on the seat!"

It was hard to hear her with the wind that whipped in; all of them had to talk so loudly they were almost yelling.

"Thanks for sharing," ground out Max.

"It's better than beetles flying into your mouth at sixty miles per hour, isn't it?" asked Hayley. Her hoodie was pulled up around her face as she cowered behind Max's seat.

"It's crap," said Max.

Cara wondered if she should try to see, again, what had frightened the birds—was it chasing them now? Was it somewhere out there in the fields spread out along the highway, somewhere in the earth beneath the road?

But she'd already had a vision, and she might need to keep her strength in reserve. She tried to think what her mother would advise.

From the front, her phone buzzed—it had charged up just enough to be notifying her of messages. She leaned forward and pulled it toward her, the charger popping out; she bent over to read it, shielding her head with her other arm.

"Wait, my phone's buzzing too," said Max. "Cara, can you check mine?"

But she didn't need to. On her screen was a group text to all of them from her mother.

It said: COLD INTERCEPTED JAX. ON TO PLAN B.

⸙

Jax was vaguely aware of lying in the back of the Subie, with a fleece blanket over him and something soft under his head. He didn't know why he had a blanket, since it was summer—and he couldn't recall being picked up by his mother, who sat in the driver's seat now. Cub wasn't in the car.

Too bad, thought Jax dreamily. He couldn't finish his job without Cub. Cub said they'd been on the brink, they'd been *in*, Cub had said. Somehow Jax had pushed right into the biggest supercomputer in the world.

He didn't remember much more. Just a sense of sharpness and metal that went on forever, as though he were in an endless library, its lights blank and bright and somehow sick, that was stacked not with books but sheaves of razor blades . . . weird. He had no idea where the image came from. Probably it stood in for something, because the internet wasn't like a big room at all and neither was the Tianhe . . . it was more like a great 3D tree of right-angled branches, like the circuit diagrams or flow charts he'd imagined the first time he pushed.

He saw the back of his mother's head when he lifted his head off the seat, a dark blur, and heard a stream of words in her voice.

". . . defenses were in place, and he was hurt. It's been repaired, for the most part, though he's still rebuilding some walls—Q came out and helped me—but there's no way I'm sending him back in. . . ."

". . . only a *baby*. No one would ask it of him. Or me. . . ."

". . . the timing. So we'll have to go in that way, forget guerrilla warfare. We have no choice but to gather . . ."

". . . the rest. From all the legions . . ."

He didn't feel so bad anymore. He was starting to warm up. He must have been in shock. Being in shock made you cold, he thought: paramedics gave people blankets in movies and TV shows. For the shock. He'd read about it— he tried lazily reaching for the file, but his head was fuzzy, so the reach trailed off. He'd gone through a phase of reading about medical emergencies, before his chess phase and after his mad-genius phase . . . it had to be in here somewhere.

Acute stress disorder: Common symptoms are: numbing; detachment; muteness; amnesia; continued re-experiencing of the event by such ways as thoughts, dreams, and flashbacks—

"Jax," came his mother's voice, softer than it had been on the phone but also clearer. No, not even her voice: her mindvoice. She was mindtalking.

I'm here, he thought.

There was no one else in the front seat, so why was she bothering?

I think it'll take less of your energy to talk this way, she said. *We haven't done it in a while, huh?*

No.

So what happened in there, do you remember?

No. I just remember razor blades, like there were millions of them. In the stacks. Instead of books.

Like a nightmare. Wasn't it.

Kind of.

OK. Don't worry. We're not sending you back in.

One of her hands came off the steering wheel and reached back to pat him gently on the arm, reassuring.

What was that? How could the, like, internet threaten me? I don't get it. I mean . . .

He didn't know how to say it, exactly.

It doesn't have agency. Like, intention. It can't do things. Right?

"Well," his mother said aloud, "we think the Cold has booby-trapped parts of the dataworld so we can't enter using the old ways. I don't know if that booby-trapping has anything to with the present action, though—we believe our knowledge of the admiral's plan is still secure—and I don't know if it was aimed at you. Although there aren't many of us who can do what you did."

"Mom," said Jax dreamily—he could talk, but it was a kind of half-asleep talking—"I've been meaning to ask. You said we only found out what the Cold was doing recently . . . I mean, that he was behind global warming. You said that, didn't you?"

"I did."

"So . . . why do we have a connection with the Cold? Like why did we, the people with old ways, find out about

103

what he was doing before—I don't know—everyone else? Regular people? Or, like, the CIA?"

"Well, we *knew* about him before they did."

"But I know *some* regular people are working with him—powerful people like the admiral . . . so some of them know, right?"

"For centuries it was only a handful of 'regular people.' That *more* than a handful of them know about him is a recent development. Their kind—the collaborators who don't have old ways, like Roger and his superiors—have always kept the Cold's existence a secret."

"Cub says he can't be an ET because the distances are too huge for that, between the stars. Cub says for sure there's life out there, but none of that life would end up reaching us here. He says no way could aliens show up from light-years away right at the moment in our history when we have the technology and civilization to even be thinking about them. He doesn't believe me."

It took a lot of effort to say all that, so he closed his eyes afterward and rested.

"He's right," said his mother. "It *was* highly unlikely. But it did occur. And the Cold has been here since before . . . well, before modern life."

"But why was it us, like, the old-ways people who knew about him before anyone else? Because . . . I mean, people don't need *our* abilities to discover things. People do a pretty good job of making discoveries without the talents we have. Galileo . . ."

"Well," said his mother slowly. "That's true, but don't underestimate how many of us are in the mainstream. Hiding in plain sight. And making some of those discoveries. Remember that book you loved when you were little? What was it called—*The Great Geniuses of the Past*? Well, many of . . . *our* kind of people were among them. And we knew about him first simply because we were around to witness his arrival. We were—well, call it culturally advanced enough, at the time, to know what we were seeing."

She was turning the wheel; Jax blinked and craned his neck to look up through the car window. He could see a piece of sky and some green road signs—they must be off the Cape now, he thought. They were on the Interstate, probably the 495. Did he know where they were going? Had she told him? Had he forgotten?

Things slipped away; things shaded into a blur.

"I don't get it."

"He came here to Earth quite a long time ago—yes. He needed a new home, because he'd used up his own. He came here and he went underground. But the old-ways people—we were around to witness it."

"It's a relief to see you all," said Mrs. Omotoso. But her eyes stayed on Zee for longer than on the others before they flicked away. It was pretty clear Zee hadn't been expected.

Cara dug around in her pocket and handed over the thumb drive.

"Excellent, Cara. Thank you. I'm just glad you made it here in one piece. Come on."

Max had driven them down and down, around and around the parking structure in Cambridge until they'd reached a level that was almost empty. They'd gotten out and stood around the car, stretching their legs and arms and waiting. It had been so battered by the flock of birds it looked like a wreck—not just the missing windshield, with its rim of small fragments all jagged around the edges and the pieces of glass lodged in the vents, but also the hood. It was a mass of scratches and dings, a pocked landscape of craters that were visible even in dimness.

There was a different entrance to the Institute now, Cara guessed, as they followed Mrs. O across the concrete floor. The way in was never the same when months went by between visits.

This time they got into an elevator, a dirty elevator that somehow smelled both metallic and grimy. Mrs. O pushed a button marked BB, and they went down farther underground and stepped out into a narrow hall. It could only fit one person at a time; Cara was on Mrs. O's heels with Hayley behind her and Zee and Max trailing. It smelled strange here too, Cara thought—like mold or mildew, something dusty and dank.

Through a door marked Custodial they squeezed, still in single file, Cara almost tripping on a yellow bucket with wheels. Then they stepped through a grate that swung open, and then they were in a place she knew.

This was the core of the Institute, with dark wood on the walls and high, arched ceilings in the larger rooms. It was full of old paintings and statues and tapestries, suits of armor in corners, curtains of brocade and velvet and walls of shelves and cubbyholes and cabinets. The lights were always gentle and dim, gleaming from sconces on the wall that looked like parchment and floor lamps whose shades were stained glass.

Even though the Institute's wards had been breached before, when the Burners attacked Cara and Hayley and Jaye, it still felt like a deep and solid place.

Mrs. O turned around and raised her hands in a welcoming gesture. "Come in and meet the others."

Jax had been half dozing when the car stopped, his head swimming with the implications of what his mother had told him, so it was nice when she picked him up, still bundled in the blanket, and carried him. It was dark around them. He was so heavy, he thought, for her to carry him, and then he realized she was carrying him as though he were almost weightless, and that was when he also realized she wasn't in her usual form at all.

His mother lumbered along in whatever dark place they found themselves—she'd said it was *somewhere safe*. She was in a furry form that didn't have the best BO. It had a skunky scent, and her breath wasn't exactly minty either. It smelled like rotten berries, maybe. Or old fish.

Yep, his mom usually smelled better than this. And typically her chest wasn't so hairy, either.

"Mama Bear," he mumbled, barely bothering to open his eyes. "For real."

She was loping along on three legs, one front leg holding him under her remarkably well, the strong, broad length of it like a cradle. Even his head was supported.

It felt nice, he had to admit, being carried by a bear you could trust.

Except for the stench. Admittedly.

"No offense, but you stink, Mom," he said.

Something rumbled in her large, warm frame. Maybe a bear could laugh, if the bear was also your mother.

Four

The Institute's cathedral-like library—which, last time Cara saw it, had been silent and empty except for her and the book she was returning—was full. A hum rose from the crowds that stood and sat around in the clawfoot armchairs and on the ancient, high-backed settees.

But the crowds weren't made of people.

Or at least, they weren't *all* people.

Behind her someone gasped, Hayley or Zee.

"It's like the *Star Wars* cantina scene," muttered Max.

"Some are fighters, others are refugees," said Mrs. O.

Cara picked out various animals she recognized among some that she really didn't—including what looked like a wolf, a mangy-looking creature like a raccoon or a possum, and a reddish-colored ape. The ape looked serious but also comic, like most great apes, as it stood beside a short old man with a white beard; it stuffed some food in its mouth from a platter on one of the long library tables, nodding as it chewed.

The way its head bobbed up and down made it look like it was considering something seriously, weighing both sides of an important decision.

There were also shapes that weren't animals or people— creatures she didn't recognize. Above a table, a circle of small lights moved like fireflies, but from where she stood she couldn't see any more than the lights; a woman who passed among the crowds like a caterer, holding up a round tray of food, had wings folded on her back that didn't look at all like a costume.

She recalled what her mother had told her about the selkie they'd met—some real creatures became mythic, part of the stories of history. Now they were called fantasy, but some of them—*some* of them—really existed.

And one man in a far corner stood so tall and thin he could hardly be a man at all.

"Fighters and refugees?" asked Hayley. "Like—refugees from where?"

"The war, of course," said Mrs. O. "And you are too. Though maybe not as directly. Most of the refugees here have been injured and are recovering."

"Is that ape an orangutan? I mean—a normal orangutan?" whispered Hayley.

"Depends what you mean by normal," said Mrs. O. "In Sumatra he went by another name, which he says Americans can't pronounce. Here he goes by Shelley. He likes romantic poetry, so he named himself after the long-dead poet."

Max guffawed.

"He's family," said Mrs. O, "but fair warning, he's an excellent mindtalker *and* a great mindreader, and he can be really obnoxious. One time he wouldn't stop sending me the text of 'Ozymandias.' It was like mental spam. *Look on my works, ye Mighty, and despair!*"

A brief, deep *Ee-yew* sound came from across the room, and Mrs. O shook her head. "Plus he reads anyone's mind he wants to, without ever asking. Pings, as you and Jax would say."

Cara felt something push against her leg and looked down: a cat walking on hind legs, wearing a cloth draped over its head.

"No way," said Max. "That's not—"

The cat on two legs tottered past them and was gone.

"So *cute!*" squealed Hayley. "That kitty should be on Cute Overload!"

"A bakeneko," said Mrs. O, looking around the room distractedly. "It's a Japanese cat spirit."

"Spirit?" asked Cara. "Like—supernatural?"

"Legendary," answered Mrs. O. "But not any more supernatural than Max here. Or me. You all have to get rid of this idea that supernatural isn't—well, *real.* You know better already, don't you? What we call supernatural is often just less understood. Like the workings of time. Or the brain."

"So like vampires? Like in *Twilight*? Are they real too?" asked Hayley.

"Not so much," said Mrs. O, and grinned quickly before her face got serious again. "Vampires are purely fictional. There *are* creatures that live on human blood, but usually we call them *mosquitos.* Kids, could you wait here for a minute? There are a couple of things I have to do. There are snacks on the table there."

"I'm kind of disappointed," said Hayley as Mrs. O threaded her way through the crowd and blended in. "No sexy *Twilight* teens with white faces and red lips? It's not fair. Vampires are totally *hot*! I'm bummed. Seriously."

"Maybe there are some real, hot werewolves," said Max. "*Real Werewolves of Beverly Hills.* Don't give up hope, Hayley."

Hayley elbowed him, but she wasn't paying close attention: all of them were still fixated on the nonhuman members of the company. Cara felt herself staring at the orangutan. He was easier to spy on than the possum- or wolf-people only because he stood a bit taller; he wore a curious tool-belt-like-garment over what looked like cargo shorts. And nothing else.

As she watched he pulled a flat thing out of a pocket of the tool belt and started stabbing at it with one big, blunt finger. For a second she drew a blank. Till she realized it was a big smartphone, maybe a small tablet. He was typing.

She heard a sigh behind her and then a swish and a light thud, and something was brushing her legs again. Cat spirit? She looked down.

Zee lay crumpled on the floor, collapsed.

"Oh no!" said Max. "She's fainted! She's done this before. Help me—let's lay her down somewhere."

So they picked up Zee, her head lolling on her shoulders, and moved her to a nearby couch, whose sole occupant (some kind of pig) uncurled itself politely and jumped off the couch to give them room. It trotted away.

"Probably she wigged out," whispered Hayley as they moved a cushion under her head. "I mean the room looks like it's full of jailbreaks from the zoo. And then Mrs. O

112

goes and says with no warning that one of them's, like, a mindreader. . . ."

"Raise her legs a bit," Max told Cara as he leaned over Zee. "Like that—yeah—just like a foot in the air, and hold them there for so her feet are higher up than her head. It helps get blood back to the brain or something. She used to have me trained. I think I remember. . . ."

"Can they, like, talk?" asked Hayley. She didn't seem too interested in Zee.

"The animal ones don't talk like we do, I don't think," said Cara, sticking a cushion under Zee's foot. "At least the leatherback doesn't. She and Jax had their old-way mind-meld thing they did. But I mean, even if they *wanted* to talk, if they knew the language and all that, I don't think they have the right—you know—vocal cords and shape of the throat to make the same sounds we make. It's why it's so important they can mindtalk or mindread. They communicate that way, Jax told me, all the old-way people and the different forms. That's what Mom called them, right? *People in different forms.* But Max. Where *is* Jax?"

"He and Mom are supposed to be headed here."

Zee mumbled something, and Max leaned down close to her face to listen.

"Watch *out* for her," said Hayley sharply.

"But we're in a ward zone," said Max. "How could she possibly be a danger?"

"I just think you should watch out," said Hayley. "We don't know. Do the adults—Mrs. O and whoever—do they know who you brought in? What her, like, story is?"

"I'll tell them," said Max, a little impatiently. Zee opened her eyes and turned her head to look around; just as she did, she let out another little scream.

Shelley was standing next to Cara, clutching his big phone. On his hind legs he was a few inches shorter than she was, but he was broad. His stomach bulged out, round as a pregnant woman's.

He looked up at her expectantly.

"Uh, hi," said Cara. "Uh, Shelley. Isn't it?"

He kept staring a bit longer, then hooted.

"So you're an *o-rang-u-tan*?" said Hayley. She enunciated very clearly, as though speaking to a small child.

Shelley poked at his phone, then held it up turned to them: a text, in large type.

No Sh*t.

"Whoa," said Max.

But Hayley just giggled.

"So are you like Koko the gorilla?" she asked. "Like, you know how to use the texting keys? Or like, a hundred basic words in sign language?"

Shelley made a rude sound with his tongue and lips and texted again.

Hows this for a basic sign?

Then he held up his middle finger.

"Huh. I guess he's more like—you know. Us," said Cara.

"Well. Nice to meet you, Shelley," said Max. "Was there something you needed?"

Word frm yr Moms. Meet in the sanctum.

114

"I'm sorry, but we don't know where that is," said Cara.

Id show u, but Id have to kill u.

Just kidding. Thru the gallery. Cmon.

He shoved his phone into his tool belt, gestured with his head, and then hunkered down to lope away from them on his knuckles.

"We have to go," said Cara. "Max, bring Zee," she said over her shoulder. Zee had hoisted herself up on her cushions, though she still looked white as a sheet. Quickly Shelley moved away into the crowd.

Hayley and Cara stayed right behind him as he pushed his way through clusters of people talking, drinking, and eating. Then he jumped in a huge leap over a couch, which they had to take the long way around, and pulled ahead of them.

Cara looked over her shoulder and couldn't glimpse Max and Zee; she had to trust they could still see her. Shelley was distinctive-looking, that was for sure, but he hunkered down too close to the ground to be high-visibility.

Finally they came to a door that led to a hall she hadn't been down, and she looked back again at they went through it, hovering there and waving desperately so that Max could see her. "Max! Right through the door!" she called, as Shelley disappeared down the corridor with Hayley on his heels.

There was a row of doors they could have disappeared into, but one was still open so she went through it, leaving it open for Max and Zee. And she saw right away why he'd called it the "gallery": it was full of paintings and sculptures like the ones she remembered from the room she'd slept in the first night she ever spent here. There were old-looking portraits of animal people—*people in different forms,* she reminded herself—but also other paintings and artifacts, no different from the ones you might see in art museums.

There were medieval-looking paintings of saints and angels, old marble statuary of kings and queens; there was an elaborate miniature model of an island, like an architect's tiny rendering of a building, but beneath the lush tropical growth on top there was also the island's underneath part, a great hang of dirt into which hundreds of holes had been bored. Cara stopped at that one for a long moment, peering down into the holes to try to see the dimly lit caverns within. What lived there, in those underground mazes? She didn't have time to study it, though, she had to start walking again to keep up—for a second she thought she'd lost sight of the others.

But there, in front of a famous painting of George Washington—the one where he was standing up, wearing a black coat, and holding a sword pointing down in one hand with the other arm stretched out—stood Shelley. He was striking the same pose as Washington, though he wore his pelt of red fur instead of the black suit and was holding his phone down by his side instead of the narrow sword. Hayley was grinning at him. But when he saw Cara, he abruptly dropped his stretched-out arm, sniffing haughtily, like the joke he'd made was actually beneath him. He turned away and kept going, while Hayley gestured to Cara to hurry up.

"The art's amazing here," she said to Cara as they struggled to keep up. Shelley was incredibly swift, for a guy that practically walked on his knuckles. "I guess it's, like, reproductions. Copies, you know? Because some of these—look! That one's by Titian! The real one is in that big French museum. The Louvre? 'Girl With Mirror,' or something— my mom actually has a postcard of it on the fridge!"

"Wait, you know which paintings are in the Louvre?" asked Cara, momentarily distracted from the walls of art by the fact that Hayley had just supplied information unrelated to fashion or celebrities.

"It's on a postcard! So sue me! I take them off the fridge sometimes and read the backs of them. Mom's clients get around *way* more than she does. They send her cool-looking cards from, like, cool foreign cities. Places my moms can like only *dream* of ever going. It's kind of sad. Though I guess it's sweet they remember to send cards to their hairdresser. Hey! Shell! Wait up, dude! You're way too fast for us Homo sapiens!"

Shelley swung his head around, emitted a hoot that sounded distinctly irritable, and squatted in place. But he did wait for them, although he tapped a foot impatiently.

"I think he likes you better than me," she said under her breath to Hayley.

"Doesn't everyone?"

When they caught up to Shelley he pulled a long feather out of his tool belt and picked his teeth with its sharp end.

"Wow, Shell. That's gross," said Hayley.

He grunted and bared his teeth at her. But after Hayley turned away, Cara noticed he quickly stuffed the offending feather back in his belt and slicked back the hair on his head.

If he hadn't been an orangutan, she thought, she would have guessed he had a crush.

As Max got close to them, holding Zee by the hand, Shelley turned to a nearby painting—one Cara thought she'd seen before of a bunch of dogs around a table playing poker. He moved his hand over it in a swift circling motion Cara didn't quite follow; he grabbed the right side of the frame and pulled, and the painting opened like a door.

As Shelley stood back and let them step through—the entrance was three feet or so off the floor, since that was as far as the painting hung down, so you had to hike up one leg at a time and half climb across—Cara felt a lift of excitement. It reminded her of the windowleaf, though so far at least it wasn't magic: a portal, she thought. There were always portals in the stories she read, sometimes through time, sometimes through space, sometimes into an alternate universe. *Portal*, she thought, was just a lofty word for door—but it was a good word. *Door* was too plain a description for an opening like this, an opening that promised to lead you from one part of your life, or one part of the world, into a truly different one.

And what they stepped into *was* different.

Where they stood was at the edge of a round room whose high, high ceiling and floor and walls were made of something like clay—a warm, brown, earthen texture, all rounded edges and uneven bumps. She put out a hand and felt the grainy texture of the wall: dirt. The room had tunnels radiating out from it, on the ground floor, and above that it went up and up and up for several floors. Dug into its walls above the tunnel entrances were small rooms, all open to the center space, that reminded her of a honeycomb.

She stood gazing around; there was a soft, amber light that left a lot of details in shadow. She couldn't see much in those rooms that climbed the walls, despite the fact that they were open . . . and what happened next happened in a flash: she saw her mother, walking toward Hayley and her; Max and Zee stepped through the door on her heels; a great noise began from somewhere above, a clicking and squeaking multiplied by thousands; she looked up to see a black cloud descending, blotting out the walls and windows of the huge honeycomb of a room. . . .

Crows again? No—bats. The cloud came down toward her so fast that she gasped, and then something with tendrils or strings brushed along her face, but it passed over her and kept going and the black beating wings passed by her too, though the clicking and squeaking sounds were still all around her.

When she turned she saw a large net had been dropped on top of Zee, and Max was struggling to get part of it off his shirt, where a loose string had stuck to the fabric. It was sticky, she saw, it stuck where it fell—it had adhered to Zee somehow, so that she couldn't move.

"Here," said her mother, helping Max peel the strand off his shirt, and then Mrs. O was there too.

"I—what did you do to her?" said Max, angry. "She trusted me! I brought her here to keep her safe, not get her attacked! Get that thing off her! What are you doing?"

"You wanted to help your friend Zee," said their mother. "We understand. But Max. This isn't her."

※

From under the net Zee kept looking at them, shaking but standing stock still. Cara felt sorry for her. Whatever Cold thing had her under its spell, she was the victim.

But it was weird how her face didn't move, how she didn't frown or cry out or say anything. She just stood there shaking quickly—almost vibrating. It wasn't normal, Cara realized, staring, that quick and microscopic vibration—it almost didn't seem physically possible.

Not for a human.

"I saw what it was in the parking structure," said Mrs. O, more to Mrs. Sykes than the kids. "And I made a split-second decision to take the risk. I opened a piece of the ward to let it through. I figured it was our best chance at complete containment—to get it inside and then sequester it. But there were some nervous moments in the library. Someone could have gotten hurt if it had reverted to form in *there*."

"I don't get it," said Hayley. "She's just a kid like us until the Cold actually *activates* her. So even if she's a vessel or sleeper or whatever, if it's all warded in here, what's the danger?"

"The Cold probably *did* have your friend tethered, but you're right," said Mrs. O. "Even tethered, she wouldn't be a danger to us in here. Not unless the wards fell, the way they did that first time when you were attacked by the Burners. And in here"— she gestured to the hive-like room with its ceiling so high Cara could barely see it—"we're in the *sanctum sanctorum* now, the core of the core. In here the wards have *never* fallen."

"But the point is, this *isn't* Max's ex-girlfriend," said their mother. "At all."

She reached out into the air behind her without even looking and moved her hand as though turning a dial— and there, standing under the net with her arms hanging limply at her sides, still vibrating rapidly until the moment when she wasn't, Zee changed.

She seemed almost to melt, as Cara and Hayley looked on in horror and Max gasped beside them, clutching at his face with his hands in a gesture so panicky Cara wanted to comfort him. He kept saying *Oh no—oh no—no way*. . . . Because Zee's face and head melted and joined her shoulders; her limbs fused to her body and she sank onto the floor. She wasn't—she wasn't—she was something pink and glistening now, a wet sheen of flesh. She was the same creature Cara had seen in the earth at the electrical station—like a huge earthworm, but with those sharp-looking horns. . . .

"No way no way no way—" Max was saying, like a chant or a prayer. He was clutching the sides of his head with his hands now.

"Jabba the *Hut*," said Hayley. "I can't believe we sat in a car with that thing! And Max held *hands* with it! Max. Gross!"

"Wait," said Cara, "it's still—changing. . . ."

Now it looked like an outsize maggot or mealworm, now more like a millipede: a dog-sized, segmented creature curling and arching, trying to dig its way into the ground.

"What is she—what are they?" asked Cara, a little panicked. Had it been out hunting Jax? Or Max or her? And then been scared off by Q and turned into . . . what looked like Zee? No, the timing wasn't right. Zee had already been in the car with them when she'd called up that vision.

There must have been more than one of them.

Zee's face had looked normal—blank, sure, a little uncertain. But normal.

"Shapeshifters, like me," said her mother. "Except that they work for the Cold. And their primary form is that of an extinct arthropod: *Anomalocaris canadensis*."

"Look at the *mouth*," said Max, repulsed. The pink thing, now about the size of a dog, had a segmented body and black eyes on stalks, but its two huge, curled protrusions were as sharp as fangs.

"The birds weren't flying *away* from something," Cara told him, only realizing it as she said it. "They were attacking. They were trying to get at *it*. To protect us."

Slowly, Max sat down. Right in the middle of the floor, like his legs had turned to rubber underneath him.

"But Zee—but she used to faint like that," he muttered. "She fainted two other times, back when. . . . How'd it *know* that?"

"*Anomalo* aren't his best and brightest," said their mother, and leaned over to put a hand against his cheek. "They're mimics by nature—they look the part and can imitate the movements, though only up to a point. Luckily for us, copying personality is beyond them . . . if you'd spent more time with it, Max, you would have known. I promise you."

"But it fainted! Just like she—"

"Probably the wards all around us were sapping its strength. It's OK, honey. Anyone could have been fooled. . . ."

"But what was—what was it going to—"

"It had a target," said Mrs. O. "They're assassins, essentially. Bloodletters. They aim for an artery, usually the femoral since they're close to the ground. And they strike. They don't like an audience, though. They don't want to get caught. This one was probably waiting to get its target alone."

"Huh. I thought you said there *weren't* vampires," grumbled Hayley.

"But—Mom. I *was* alone with her before I picked up Cara and Hayley," Max protested. "See, she came to the house—I found her waiting on the front porch. Or it, I guess. And she asked me to help her. She seemed scared. I didn't know what to do. I didn't mean to put—to risk—"

"It's OK, dear. The neighborhood wards must have already been down on the bayside, or it couldn't have got that far," said their mother. "It's not your fault. You saw in it what you *wanted* to see. It's part of what they rely on."

"So why didn't she—it—just attack me then?"

"Because you weren't the target," said a voice behind them.

They turned around: Jax, looking unbearably tired.

"Jax!" said Cara—but then the creature under the net began to emit a hissing noise, louder and louder and higher and higher. It was grating and terrible—it made her wish she couldn't hear at all. Sand began to crumble off the walls; furniture shook and chittered on the ground, and somewhere something fell and shattered.

When the keening stopped, the creature lay still.

"Deathsong," said Mrs. O.

―◈―

"You can place your trust in the bats. It's not their fault they've become illness vectors—it's ours, for infringing on their territories. And you can trust the birds. Always," said their mother. They were all sitting in one of the open rooms overlooking the main hall of the sanctum.

Shelley had clambered off and scaled a ladder so fast Cara didn't see where he ended up.

"The bats and the birds are with us," agreed Mrs. O. "All of them. They always have been."

"Crows are highly intelligent," added Jax. "Some species of crows have an encephalization quotient approaching the EQ of apes."

"I totally understand everything you just said," said Hayley flatly.

Cara felt even sadder now for the birds that had died against the glass. She thought of their broken wings beating feebly as they died. *They were just trying to protect us.*

"What are these rooms *for*?" asked Hayley.

She was standing on the edge of their compartment, looking out. It wasn't easy to see what was in the other rooms; some were dark, and the ones that were lit mostly had curtains half pulled across their open sides, shadows moving behind them.

"Sanctuary, like much of this place," said their mother. "They're mini-habitats—shelters equipped to house a lot of different forms. This one was designed for people like us, but some are for water-based forms, aquaria basically. Some are mud wallows. Some are nests. Some are earth, for burrowing forms that don't feel safe in open air. One's even a small piece of pasture, if I recall correctly."

"I don't really get why you call this place an Institute," said Hayley. "It doesn't seem anything *like* a school."

"We *don't* call it that, as a matter of fact," said Mrs. Sykes. "Cara and Jax first came to it that way. But 'Institute' is a generic name for the façade. A cover that makes us invisible to the mainstream. To old-ways people this is simply a refuge, and we name our refuges for places that live on only in memory. There are hundreds of them. One's called Atlantis, another Nakbe, one Eridu. The name of this one is Thrace."

Thrace. Cara let that settle.

"So. Mom. You gonna tell us about Plan B?" asked Max.

He was still a little stunned, Cara thought. Wherever the real Zee was, she hadn't come back to him after all. She'd never showed up at their door and started talking to him again, never asked for his help.

"Two things. First, Jax and Cub's task: the Cold had more defenses in place than we're comfortable with. We can't have Jax going back in there. Second, the admiral's timetable's been moved up, which means we can't take any of the diplomatic paths. We decrypted his emails—thanks to you, Cara and Hayley—and they suggest the warhead's already in play on board a U.S. submarine. It could be launched at a position in the Mid-Atlantic Ridge as soon as . . . well. Possibly tomorrow."

There was a silence as they all looked at her, even Hayley, who'd turned from her view of the hive to gape with the rest of them.

"The nuclear—the bomb?" she asked, unbelieving.

"It's headed to the rift valley."

"So what does that—what does it mean?" asked Cara.

"Most of us here are gathered for departure. We're headed toward Ground Zero."

"*We* are?" asked Cara.

"Not all of us. Not you. I want you to stay in Thrace."

"Us who? And—stay here and do what?"

"We need Jax as a communications relay. A hub to receive and resend messages in the formats our various people understand, working with central command, which is here. I've already talked about it with him. He needs to be safe and warded to do that work, so he can't go out with us into the middle of the ocean. Cara, you may be able to help him by summoning—that's not clear yet. But either way, I need you here to keep an eye on him; he's still recovering from the Cold's cyberattack. And Hayley, we're going to be asking you to help with the wounded."

"The wounded? Me? *What* wounded?"

"The wounded from Ground Zero, of course. Believe me. They'll be arriving all too soon."

"But—"

"You'll work with our healers in the solarium. You should have some ability in that realm. You'll assist Mr. Sabin. And Max? You're coming with me."

Cara turned and wandered to the room's edge, where she stood looking over the great cavernous air space of the hive.

You could step off, she thought, and just fall. They were only on the second floor now, but those rooms at the top were six stories up. It'd be suicide if you stepped out of a room near the top . . . and just as she pictured that and shivered, she saw a shadow swoop out of a high room. It flitted back and forth, a silhouette against the faint lights of the faraway ceiling.

Those high-up rooms must be only for forms that flew, she realized. There were no stairs to get up there; there was no elevator either.

Not a problem to fall if you had your own wings.

Jax had come up beside her.

"You know, Mom isn't giving Max these—adult jobs, if you like, because he's smarter than you or more mature. She just wants to keep him close."

She looked at her little brother. He had bags under his eyes that hadn't been there before. His face looked so tired.

"What happened to you, Jax?"

"I'll tell you when I can," he said.

⚎

But privately Jax wasn't sure about his older brother with his emergent, possibly dangerous talent that no one knew about. He thought about urging Max to tell their mother, at least—now, before they left. Before they went out there, to wage their battle in the deep blue sea.

When he thought of it he felt a stab of fear.

He couldn't show it, though. Because even if he *was* the little brother, even if he *was* the irritating kid who stuck on Max's heel like an old piece of gum, he was also the kid who knew things. Even his brother often respected what he knew—or half respected, at least.

So his doubt might have the power to scare them. If he acted afraid then other people would be too. His fear would be contagious.

He'd snuck off to the library while the others talked, feeling a pull from the multiple streams of mindtalk twisting and weaving there. Crowds had amassed around the long library tables, images floating over them and rippling the air. There was urgency and adrenalin in the room that made itself felt right along with the thoughts; it trembled in the air. He didn't want to be observed by all those people he didn't know, he just wanted to listen, so he sat down in the shadows of an alcove that housed a looming white statue of a giant octopus (*Enteroctopus dofleini*, he guessed).

He sat cross-legged in the space beneath the gracefully curving tentacles and slowed his heartbeat. They were talking and thinking so fast, and in such complicated threads of back-and-forth, that he had to teach himself how to separate the strands from each other. The conversation had acquired volume, somehow, if not mass—it was like a great, twisting cloud that filled the air of the massive room. It hung there above their heads, impossibly huge and hulking, a kind of looming storm of energy.

But now and then he had to pull himself out of the tangle abruptly. It was shot through with grim threads, with gray-black, ashy knots of warning and trepidation. Here he caught sight of a calculation, for instance: the numbers of possible casualties, the number of fatalities. Here he saw a scenario if they failed: fallout carried slowly through the deep ocean, then along the Gulf Stream, the North Atlantic Drift. He caught the edges of memories: the nuclear explosions, hundreds of them that had once, during the decades

of the Cold War, killed many creatures that swam inno-
cently among the warm atolls of the Pacific, that roamed
the far, wild reaches of cold Siberia. Some of the thinkers
had known creatures killed by these tests, places poisoned
by them. He felt their old grief in snatches and shuddered
when it hit.

The gray-black strands were specters of harm and
death, visions of ruined places both under the sea and on
land.

He had to bring up his shields and shut it off. Maybe he
was just a baby, he thought, blinking back tears at the sights.

And maybe he needed to save his strength.

So he settled the shields in place and sealed himself off
neatly. He was taking a break. Yeah: for a few minutes he
would pretend he was a normal kid. He uncrossed his legs
and got up—free of overhearing, free of interpretation, free
of *knowledge*—and strolled along the perimeter of the old
library.

It *was* relaxing. He heard only the regular ambient
sounds that anyone could hear. People shuffled around,
there was the occasional spoken exclamation or burst of
argument, trailing off into silence again as they fell back
into mindtalk. There were chairs scraping back, doors clos-
ing, old grandfather clocks ticking in a deliberate, satisfying
way, their brass pendulums slowly swinging. He let himself
gaze at the artifacts on display and almost felt the weight lift
from his shoulders. He even pretended his father was with
him and they were in a regular museum.

Hey, Dad, look there, what is that? The clay tablets of Persia? Really? What's that rock—what? The Sphinx's beard? I thought you told me that was stowed away in storage in the basement of the British Museum! What kind of skull is that? Australopithecus?

But before long the people in different forms had finished their conference and were milling and rushing around. A fair number left the room to gather weapons from an "armory" (he heard one of them say it aloud). T minus one hour—he had to snap back into it, he knew, as the clutch of planners broke apart to make their separate preparations, so he dropped his shields for long enough to key into the battle plan. The skein of ideas had untangled and settled in their minds and he was able to skim through and pick up the details.

His phone dinged: a text from Cara. SIT WHERE I CAN SEE YOU. IT'S SUPERCROWDED.

Somehow, he realized sheepishly, he'd expected the throng to beam where they were going—like in *Star Trek*, Cub's favorite nerdly show. He'd actually half-expected them to simply dematerialize. Cara'd told him that once, when she first came to the Institute to help him and he got hollowed out, someone had phased through a wall with him. Mrs. Omotoso, maybe. Of course, he had no memory of it at all.

He really didn't know where old-way technology stopped. He didn't know its limits. So far, whenever he tried a new door, it opened.

More crowds poured in, gathering under the dome. Cara and Hayley waved to him from one of the smaller doors—he'd perched atop a heavy old bookshelf that gave him a good view—and pushed their way through the throng. The tables and overstuffed furniture had sunk into the floor or been moved aside to make room for the *forms*, now exposed in their full and different glory. It could have been an Ark if there'd been two of everything—and if the Ark had included glittering, horse-sized lizards that might as well be called dragons and bears that had to be grizzlies and buzzing insectoid creatures, tiny and highly intelligent, that from far away bore a startling resemblance to lit-up Tinkerbells. . . .

Packed in with all these bright and odd beings, plain old people were suddenly in the minority—there were lumbering mammals, there were swarms of butterflies and bees, there were gnome-like women barely taller than toddlers. Just as Cara and Hayley made it to his bookshelf he felt a huge power drain. Lights winked out around them, the air-conditioning ceased, and the few computer screens around the library walls went black—every joule of nearby energy was being used, somehow harvested for the transformation, because as the lights came on again, one by one, slowly, he could see the crowd had changed.

"The shapeshifters," breathed Cara. "They're getting ready for flight."

And it was true: anyone who could shapeshift had taken the same flying form, so that now it looked as though a great flock of oversized seabirds were massed under the dome. Like huge seagulls, Jax thought—or no! like the wandering albatross, which could have up to twelve-foot wingspans, even bigger than condors. But these were even bigger and heavier than that, because as he stared *people* were climbing onto their backs, and not only people but other creatures Jax couldn't quite make out.

The lights still wavered and flickered; it was still dim.

"It's Max! Max is riding one of them!" cried Hayley, pointing, and they watched as Max adjusted himself on the back of his massive white bird, leaning forward over its neck like a jockey on a racehorse.

Cara wondered if the bird was her mother.

Then in a sudden hush one of the dome's sides dropped, opening the great room to the night sky. And in the sky a vast window opened, which at first was indistinguishable from the sky itself: a black scene of water beneath the stars.

"Like the windowleaf," said Cara beside him. "Another portal."

The flock raised its wings and took off, the front lines first, the middle and rearguard following—they entered the scene flying, and some dove straight away into the ocean while others flapped away into the sky.

"The ones who dove are changing *again*," said Cara. A few of the albatrosses had become fish or sharks or other large aquatic creatures that were too far away to be clearly visible, diving down with their passengers clinging to their backs.

Jax watched the crowds disappear into the scene, a faint music playing as they grew farther and farther away. He didn't know where it was coming from, or if the others heard it.

"Mom told me they would shift like that," said Cara. "They have to shift a bunch of times. This part of the fight—this army here—it's shifters and fighters and a few communicators. The fighters are the riders, and they have weapons, and the communicators can ping and talk and all that. . . ."

The crowds thinned out, vanishing into the seascape beyond. Jax glanced sidelong at the few people who remained, trying not to be noticed, and decided they were people and creatures who might be unfit for a fight. Most were either too old or too young or injured refugees—in a corner he saw a bird he thought was a swan, cradling a broken wing. Some were medical staff: he saw Mr. Sabin standing over a small console on the wall. Mr. Sabin was adept in the old-way medicine that used light to heal wounds and cure disease; he'd have stayed behind to take care of the wounded.

With the room almost emptied, the strange, great flock scattered, Jax followed Cara and Hayley over to a globe on a pedestal, which they were idly spinning on its axis. It was a large, gold-colored globe that looked antique and remarkably different from the globes he was used to, having different skins you could slide back like the layers of an onion. . . .

Then he smelled something not very good, like ketchup mixed with sweat, and turned and looked over his shoulder.

The orangutan.

The guy was way too close for comfort, maybe six inches from Jax's face, and was eating pizza, which he chewed with his mouth fairly wide open. Meanwhile he glared at Jax balefully. They were almost exactly the same height.

His mom had told him about this guy.

"You must be Shelley," he said. "Hi."

Shelley chewed and stared Jax down. Then he thought aggressively.

And you must be the boy wonder. Big whup.

Jax didn't have the energy to ping him back.

"Hey. Are you supposed to help me? Or insult me?"

Can't I do both?

The orangutan swallowed a last bite of pizza, reached out, and wiped his greasy fingers slowly and heavily right down the middle of Jax's shirt.

They left large stripes of pizza sauce.

"Whuh—? Hey! What'd you do *that* for?"

Uh, didn't have a napkin. Obviously.

"Wait. Is Shelley *pinging* you?" broke in Cara.

Jax looked up to see that, just then, the last remnants of the strange battle-crowd were disappearing into the dark frame; a last, lone flapping of wings caught Jax's eyes and he watched, transfixed, as the scene faded and the dome's wall moved up again, sea and stars quietly vanishing.

"He's *totally* pinging me," he told his sister, turning away from the dome when he realized he was staring at a blank wall. "And he's kinda mean."

"Play nice, Shell," scolded Hayley. "Jax is the baby of the family. He's only eleven!"

So what? I'm only twelve myself. But I'm gettin' my cheek flaps soon.

He thought it with an actual *swagger*. Jax hadn't known that was even possible.

"Uh. He says he's only twelve himself," reported Jax politely. "And something about cheek flaps?"

"Wait. If he can mindtalk to you, how come he has to use that giant phone to talk to *us* with? Mom mindtalks to me sometimes, and I don't have any of those telepath talents," said Cara, curious.

I don't ping girls, thought Shelley at Jax. *That's gross.*

"Um, he says . . . he wouldn't want to intrude on the, uh, ladies," offered Jax.

Shelley rolled his eyes.

"Well, anyways," said Hayley, "if you're twelve, you're a younger man, Shell. You're barely older than Jax! So I have to say no to that date you asked me on. I don't date the little guys."

Shelley already had his phone out, which he held up to Hayley.

THATS 35 IN RANG YEARS.

"Mmm. Still," said Hayley. "Gotta pass. I'm exclusive. I only date my own species."

THEN SHUT UP AND FOLLOW ME.

There was so much, Jax thought as he tagged along after his obnoxious fellow primate, that he needed to think about, that he needed to tell the others—great secrets, vast secrets. But when?

It was never the right time, he thought, in the middle of a war.

Five

This was the communications room, Cara guessed, what her mother had called the *deepscreen room.* It had a big, round table in the middle, then a ring of computers outside that, screens running along the walls. Too many to count. The screens were lit up with moving images, complex maps that showed the weather along with other movements beneath the clouds—like the radar weather on TV if you combined that with a regular view of the Earth from satellite and could see it all moving.

Beside those screens were others that showed live feeds of the ocean at night, dark, glittering expanses with a few faint lights above that might be stars. Even better, there were feeds from *under* the waves, like views from one of those submersibles you saw in TV shows about life under the ocean. The scenes weren't dark, even though it was full night outside; they were lit by a yellow-green glow she imagined must be lights on the cameras themselves. Vague shapes floated across them, then disappeared. Those feeds had to be from close to Ground Zero.

She wondered if the screens were portals too. Could she step right into one, step right through its frame into another place, as the legions had, flying out of Boston and into the middle of the Atlantic . . . ?

Trying not to look obvious, she approached the nearest screen and stuck out a hand tentatively.

Nope. It might be a deepscreen to some, but to her it was solid. Still, the *image* on it was like the image of Ananda they'd seen on her mother's old monitor at home—it had a strange quality of being present, the feeling of three dimensions instead of two. Wait. Did it almost *smell* like the ocean. Or was she making that up?

Shelley had lost interest in them as soon as he brought them here, loping over to talk to a tall man in the corner—a man so tall, it seemed to Cara, he wasn't quite human. It wasn't just his height either; it was his oddly shaped head, which looked more like the head of a grasshopper and sat forward on his shoulders at an angle. He didn't have much of a neck. She couldn't see all the details, though, because his head was attached to a whole bunch of lit-up threads, like cables, that connected to a device he was using with one of the screens.

She didn't want to stare too long so she pretended to be interested in what Hayley was doing—hovering in front of one of the screens with a satellite view on it, zooming in and out again using the touchpad and trying to figure out what she was looking at. Meanwhile, a few feet away, Jax was being schooled in how to use another piece of equipment by the short old man with the white beard they'd first seen talking to Shelley.

Then Mr. Sabin was standing in the open door, a couple of men behind him in what looked a lot like scrubs.

"Hayley? Come with me, please," he called, beckoning her away from the map. "We're headed to the sickbay. Don't have casualties yet, but it won't be long."

"But—I don't know *anything* about being an EMT—I mean all I know is a little CPR," protested Hayley nervously. "And that's just because we had to learn it for swim team."

"Don't worry," said Mr. Sabin, and nodded briskly at the white-bearded man.

"But Mr. S, I'm not even that *good* at it. It creeped me out, putting my lips on the like *open mouth* of the blowup dummy. I can't imagine it with a real live *human*. That has bad *breath* maybe? And *saliva*?"

"Trust me," said Mr. Sabin. "You'll have a latent ability in the healing arts. Despite your highly convincing appearance of total incompetence."

"See you," grumbled Hayley to Cara, kicking the floor with a toe before she reluctantly followed him out.

Before long Jax was set up at a terminal; beside him, along the row of screens, sat others. Not all the screens had keyboards either; one had only a weird kind of touchpad suspended on delicate threads—and on closer inspection Cara saw moths were flitting around the strings, vibrating them. The longer she watched, the more it looked like the moths were flying in patterns, patterns that looked almost like a dance.

Moths, she thought. *Pinch me.*

What could she contribute compared to dancing moths or her brother the prodigy? Or the rest of them, either, hunched over their monitors with laser-like focus?

"Cara? I may need your vision when I can't pull up a scene on the monitors," he said. "If I do, I'll ping you something like—show the northeast corner. Or, show the legion on the west flank. I'll be talking about one of these areas on the grid, all of them near Ground Zero. See?"

He pulled up a map on his screen, divided into numbered areas.

"So when I ping, I'll send some content with it. Like if it was Sector 4, and I want to see what's going on there, I'll send you a visual of the map, and the hope is that could be enough for you to bring up a picture."

"That's so advanced," she said. "I've never—"

"I know. Just do what you can."

She nodded, though she felt a yawning pit of anxiety in her stomach—what if she couldn't clear her mind around all these people? Everything hinged on that.

She gazed down the line of terminals beyond Jax, down the row of people and animals working at their stations. There was a very small woman, not like the terrible crone from the deserted house in Orleans but cheery and gnomelike; there were the moths, tracing their delicate patterns around the wires and the monitor; there was the tall man with his mantis head; and then Shelley, typing furiously with his tongue sticking out of his mouth in concentration.

She was *so* out of her league.

"Jax, I can't—I have to be in a quiet place," she said urgently. "It'll be too *hard* for me, standing here with all these strangers around, right in the middle of everyone.

So—you can still ping me if I'm at the other end of the room, can't you?"

"Sure—and don't worry so much. Worrying won't help you. In fact, it'll probably make your job harder."

Your honesty is not helpful, she thought.

But Jax's eyes were already on the map on his screen, where he was watching the movement of masses of twinkling lights in the dark.

"What are they doing, exactly? Do you know their plan?" she asked.

"It's complex—a much larger force than what we saw here. The legions are gathering from all over—there are tens of thousands there already. And there are decoys too, guerrilla teams going in from nether spaces—"

"But what are they doing? I mean, what's the goal?"

"One legion's focused on getting physical control of the warhead. That's an underwater op directed at the admiral's flagship sub. Then another flank's going after the command structure. . . ."

She shouldn't have asked. She had to focus on her small piece, or she would never clear her mind. Focus on what *she* could do.

So she waved at Jax and moved away, prowling the edges of the room until she found a door that opened into a closet. It was nothing special, just a small, shallow closet full of wires and electronics, blinking lights and switches and stacks of metal boxes. But no one else was around, and to her it looked like a safe haven. If she moved a heavy box aside with her foot, there was just enough room for her to sit cross-legged on the floor; and if she left the door cracked open, Jax, turning his head to one side, would be able to see her, just barely. She was near enough for a ping.

So she sat and closed her eyes and tried to make her mind tranquil.

※

Jax held his fingers on the touchpad and kept his eyes on the deepscreen in front of him. The mindtalk, as it crossed back and forth over the battlefield of the dark ocean, was his to monitor and sometimes direct, when the vectors weren't strong enough to get where they should be going. He was a signal booster and air-traffic controller rolled into one, his mother had said. He could keep the arcs of thought moving toward their target allies; he pictured their trajectories and smoothed them forward with his mind, making sure the streams connected as quickly and cleanly as they could.

The thought-traffic patterns reminded him of *Spirographs,* those looping, flower-patterned drawings you could do by putting your pen in a hole in a plastic disc and moving the disc around in different patterns. Curving lines crossed each other in such dense concentrations that they looked like intricate and graceful birds' nests. The problem was, he saw them best when he closed his eyes, but of course he couldn't look at the deepscreen with closed eyes.

So he changed out the scene on the screen with a live map, where the forces showed up in thermal imaging. He brought up inset video frames in all the corners, wanting to see multiple scenes at once. He had an idea that if he knew, at least a bit, what actual features people's thoughts referred to, it would be easier to manage them.

Now he had a view of the admiral's submarine, its round-nosed length moving through the water like a sinister black bullet—no coincidence, he thought, that submarines looked like outsize torpedoes, torpedoes like miniaturized submarines. The camera was stuck to the submarine's skin like a rearview mirror, somehow, so that all he could see was one side of the sub receding into the dark fathoms. There must be a light somewhere, because he could see the curve of the metal hulk and an occasional dim feature in the background, even though the submarine was deep in the dark waters of the ocean and it was night.

Then there were the sub's insides. That camera had to have gone undetected too—maybe because it was up so high, apparently on a ceiling. Good to know the legions even had spies *inside* American nuclear subs . . . or maybe not so good, he admitted, depending how it made you feel about so-called "national security."

The camera was in the control room. It must be so claustrophobic in there—under those heavy layers of water, with no windows, only machines. From the view on the ceiling he looked down at the tops of sailors' heads as they hunched over their monitors and occasionally stood up to move around briefly, then sat down again.

For the moment, at least, the interior feeds weren't exciting.

His third view was of a deep undersea scene near Ground Zero, at a position that was the closest the allies had gotten so far. It showed a spume of gas coming out of the seafloor between what looked like rocky canyon walls. For a few minutes he couldn't pinpoint the light source, until he realized the scene's ambient lighting had to come from bioluminescence—like the red tide of algae that he and Cara had dived in off Marconi Beach when they faced the Pouring Man near the shipwrecked *Whydah*. He couldn't be sure of the source of the luminosity, but the light was diffuse and the rocks themselves shone faintly in a way that he guessed could only be organic.

And finally there was a view from the ocean's surface, not unlike the view they'd had when the flocks of albatrosses lifted off through the dome—the moon shining on water, a couple of dark, hulking ships in the distance. These were U.S. warships under the admiral's orders, he knew. They were behemoths, but so far they were dark—instead of shining with lights, as such ships must usually be at night, they were barely visible over the sea. They were in some kind of stealth mode.

Now the legions were converging in a wide ring around all the elements of the scene, around the cruiser and destroyer—he'd never have known the difference without the stray thoughts he was catching and boosting.

In a jolt he felt a wall of chaotic thought as the first battle was joined. He could almost make it out through the screen of other people's awareness, a sense of struggle, a sense of two masses forced against each other. It was so fast—it was happening in the sky above the water, he thought, because he felt the sudden plummet of a great, shapeshifted albatross into the sea. And then the slowing and fading of its heartbeat.

There were elementals out there whose presence felt like a stream of viciousness pouring out into the night, though what weapons were being used wasn't clear. The weapons were light and energy, as far as Jax could tell. Not projectiles. But another albatross fell, and then another. He felt them wink out like stars.

The creatures of the Cold. Jax couldn't tell what they were—they were formless, except for the parts that were sharp and tore, either talons or great hard maws like beaks. He caught pieces of the suffering inflicted by those sharp parts, suffering that flew up into the night almost as tangible as impact—thoughts that were nothing but waves of feeling, yet still struck the sky and the mind in a kind of violence.

This flank is already losing, he thought. We're *losing.*

He shuddered and grimly tried to absorb it, because if he didn't it might knock him out too. Then he would be useless to all of them.

We need our *own* in the water, he thought, and could hear others thinking it too, begging abjectly in a way that radiated out from the hurt ones and the dying. He had to help them call.

He opened his eyes and squinted hard at the video feed from the ocean, but it was too black. He couldn't *see* the fight at all, he could only gather its thoughts.

But Cara could.

Even though she was expecting it, the first ping from Jax still came as a shock. He wanted to see something, wanted to see part of the fight, where the great birds were falling into the water and being—

She shook it off. She needed to know *just* enough to ask. So she did, she squeezed her eyes shut and gritted her teeth and pushed other thoughts and ideas away as forcefully as if they were real objects.

And she surprised herself, relief rushing in as a scene sprang into life behind her eyelids. It was a scene she hoped Jax was getting, Jax with his amazing, complex ability to read . . . but the second after she felt the elation of success, she felt sick.

Because the albatrosses were falling. When they fell their riders tumbled off, and though she saw one change as it hit the water—it was a shark, suddenly, not an albatross anymore—the riders couldn't change, *they* weren't shapeshifters and they couldn't fly, and so they crashed into the water and had to swim. She couldn't tell what they were swimming toward, only that they were trying to reach safety. Some albatrosses tucked their wings and floated on the surface as the riders clung to them . . . but then out of the deep water came *others*.

They appeared first as whiteness spreading on top of the water, then pinkness, dark red—giant squid or octopi?

No, not exactly. The attackers were stranger and more lethal. She saw sharp, thin appendages rise and come down on the birds, on the swimmers—tentacles, talons, she wasn't sure, but the rest of their bodies floated jellylike and stretched on and on over the surface. And their talons tore up the birds in front of her eyes.

The albatrosses' feathers flew even as they tried to shift forms themselves, and they fell and sank and died.

There are too many of the others, she thought. *There aren't enough of us. . . .*

She would have closed her eyes to block it out, only they were already closed, of course. Instead she felt a shock like white light inside the lids; maybe she jerked back, because she felt something hit the back of her head too. Then she felt Jax reaching away from her, taking his ping somewhere else, and the scene of the attack faded, though it left an odd ache behind.

Of powerlessness, because she'd seen it but she couldn't do anything about it. That was the down side of visions. If seeing was the only talent you had, you had to be satisfied with it—it had to be enough just to see.

But it wasn't.

Though the vision was gone she still had its memory: the bird floating with its tucked wings, peaceful as a dove, then torn apart. The jellies sinking under the surface again.

She sat feeling shocked all over, as though someone had taken a massive hand and slapped her whole body.

He could do it, he knew—he just had to sweep over the southern flank of the legions and he could send them in the right direction to help the fallen.

But he couldn't make the call. His job was just to filter the threads of need to the southern legion's command so the *leaders* could make the decision. He knuckled down and helped move the thought stream to the south to connect.

He knew when it was being received, and he got an answer right away: They couldn't be spared. The southern legion was fully occupied, swarming over the submarine—so thick on its metal hide that, when he looked at the screen, he couldn't see it anymore for the animals that covered and surrounded it. Their bodies caught the light only for brief flashes, so Jax saw mostly flanks and fins and tails. He thought he saw a frilled shark, and a beautiful, reddish creature shaped like a bell: a vampire squid.

To the north, somewhere in the dark, the great birds were still falling, falling as though shot through the heart.

Max, thought Cara, watching the fall of birds. Her mother. Her mother had been in an albatross form, and Max had been riding one. Was he one of the people struggling in the icy cold water? If her mother hadn't already fallen, was she about to right now? Would they be floating on the dark water with those others coming up slowly from beneath?

She had to help Max, she thought, and her mother—
she *had* to.

"Jax!" she cried out from her closet.

I'm trying, said Jax in her mind. *I'm trying.*

But he couldn't find Max's mind. Way too far away to ping,
and he could never pick through the thousands of thought
threads fast enough to find them. . . .

Cara, he thought. *Cara, I need you again. You have to
bring up a vision of them,* he pinged. *Of where exactly they
are. What their—what state they're in. Then maybe we can
do something to help. Or at least...at least we'll know what
should be done.*

But she was terrified by that; something in her revolted.
What if they were hurt? What if—?

And anyway she couldn't clear her mind—she still tin-
gled with the shock of seeing the spreading, jellylike masses
coalesce from below, the flash of their long talons. A gray-
and-white wing floating, spread out on the surface.

And that could be her mom and Max. It might already
have been—no. She shut out the thought, angry.

It was too much.

She sat trembling on the floor of the closet, cross-legged,
her hands clenched into fists on her knees.

I can't, Jax, she thought. *I want to help but I can't do that!*

Come on, pinged Jax, *come on. I can't help them, I have to
keep doing this—but you can. You can help them.*

"No," she said out loud. "I can't!"

She sprang up from the closet, not thinking about what she was doing, pushed the door all the way open, and dashed across the room and out. Then she was running down the hall so hard she didn't even have time to breathe. *Get me out.* She ran past the door to the gallery, past an elevator, down a corridor she hadn't been down before, and she kept going, turning corners and starting to breathe again, panting hard as she flashed past doors that were open, rooms lit inside, full of people. The rooms were full of equipment too, full of screens, full of lit-up displays, full of turning images that looked like the holograms in sci-fi movies; they were full of weird instruments she didn't recognize.

But even more than that: people. She slowed to a jog as she started to realize how *many* people were inside the rooms, through the doors. So many people, and people in other forms, all of them working, all of them helping—she couldn't even tell what they were doing, but it dawned on her that the small room she and Jax had been in was only one room among dozens.

Among hundreds, maybe.

And then she found herself peering around a doorjamb into a room full of blue light, where moving lines like lasers streamed over cots lined up against the wall. People stood around the beds making the lights move, the way they had over Jax so long ago, the first time she ever came to the Institute.

Only this time one of the people—in a white, baggy cotton gown like a surgeon would wear and a mask over her mouth—was Hayley.

And there was something completely new about her, something Cara had never seen before.

She moved her hands through the air over a wounded person—Cara stepped through the door and then edged closer to see—and soft threads of lights moved out of the palms and joined other threads of light, in slightly different shades and shapes, from other healers standing around the bed with her. But the light coming from Hayley's hands wasn't even what stopped Cara; it was her friend's eyes that were different, or maybe the way she held herself.

With the light beams dappling her, the way she was standing beside the bed, hands raised, a sad but somehow peaceful expression in those eyes—she looked unlike the Hayley Cara had always known.

"Good," said the man next to her. "Smitty, you do the pressure. Everyone else, ten minutes' rest."

The healers fell back and Hayley finally glanced up and saw Cara. She peeled off her mask as she walked, and her face reset itself in a familiar expression, like she was resuming her regular identity.

"How did you *do* that?" asked Cara, amazed. "How'd you know how?"

"It's not even hard!" said Hayley. "Seriously. Mr. S showed me and I was kind of, like, making fun of the idea that him showing me light coming out of his hands could do anything to help *me* with it. Like how Jax docs calculus in his head but I can't even get the times tables right in mine. So I was all, 'Neat trick, Mr. S, but um . . .' And I was making fun of it, right? So I moved my hands in this goofy way in the air, you know? Kind of imitating him, but mocking. But then. . . ."

"Then what?"

"Then it worked."

Cara gazed at her. She was confused—she'd somehow thought the old ways were only in her family. Or at least, that they couldn't randomly show up in her best friend.

"That's—how can that even *be*?" she asked. Visions didn't come half as automatically.

"Probably anyone can do it," shrugged Hayley. "Probably Mr. S like hypnotized me to be able to imitate him. Or something. Like telepathically taught me. I mean, they totally do that stuff."

Cara walked closer to the patient the healers had been treating—a man who looked perfectly healthy to her, except that he was very pale. A faint pulse beat in a vein on his temple.

"What was—what was wrong with him?"

"He'd been electrocuted somehow," said Hayley. "I don't know everything in the diagnoses—I just follow their lead. I give them energy, and they direct it however they need to, for the healing. Like laser surgery, except on an even smaller scale, Mrs. S said. I'm like a battery. That's how Mr. S described it, anyhow. You don't have to know anything about the medical side to do that. But honestly? I kind of really dig it!"

Cara turned slowly and looked at the next cot, behind her. On it lay an albatross almost the size of a person, its eyes closed.

She looked up at Hayley, who just shook her head. The two of them stared at the still, enormous bird, its wing folded alongside it.

Cara felt tears gathering at the bottoms of her eyes.

"Is that its—what's its true form?" she asked, a little choked up.

She was thinking: *What if it's—*

Mr. Sabin was at her shoulder.

"He was no one you know," he said gently, and pulled a sheet carefully up over the sleek head. "His primary form wasn't one you're even familiar with. But he was a true friend."

The three of them stood quietly for a minute. Cara thought she'd never seen anything as beautiful as the dead bird.

Or as sad.

"Is my mom—is Max—do you know if they're . . . ?"

"We have to be patient," said Mr. S, and patted her on the shoulder.

"Wait," said Hayley, and cocked her head. "How come you're not in that room with Jax? Aren't you supposed to be helping him?"

That brought Cara back to earth—a heavy guilt.

She shook her head, unable to say anything.

"Go back," said Mr. S, kindly but firmly. "Your brother needs you."

Something rang on the wall—a bell or an alarm—and he walked quickly toward it.

"Come on," said Hayley, and grabbed Cara's arm. "I'll walk you. I've got another five minutes to rest up. Batteries have to recharge, right? All the healers take breaks. There's a rotation."

Just as they passed through the door, the wall where the bell had rung opened into blackness and Cara stole a peek back at what was coming through: a seal, one flipper dragging and bleeding, that morphed, as it came, into a limping man. But Hayley pulled her away.

"But I can't *do* it," she told Hayley as they rushed along the hall. She wasn't even sure they were going in the right direction, but Hayley was steering her and was confident. "He wants me to summon a vision of Mom and Max, and what if they're—or what if I can't do it, and then it's my fault that the worst happens to them? You saw—I mean . . ."

Hayley's hand pressed hers firmly and warmly, and surprisingly she felt a wave of calm radiate from where their two hands touched.

It was almost like a wave of heat, it felt so real.

"Did you do that on purpose?" she asked.

"Do what?" asked Hayley, and before Cara had even registered how long it was taking them, there they were, at the door. Jax was hunched over his screen, as were the others in his row; the room was quiet except for the sounds of typing and the faint hum of the monitors.

"Oh—never mind . . ." trailed off Cara. She found she felt better, she felt stronger, and it didn't matter, right now, how that had come to be.

Maybe it was just her mood lifting.

But anyway, she could do this. She could try. Jax wanted her to, and Jax had to know she wasn't any kind of expert.

"See you later," whispered Hayley, and squeezed her hand good-bye before letting go.

⚏

It was almost a trance he was in, though he was sticking to his mother's rule not to push anywhere he didn't need to go—to stay on the battlefield, to stay in the netherspace where he could receive and manipulate transmissions. Still he did feel, in almost the same way he'd felt at the library, the concrete physical space around him fade away while the space in his mind became the whole world.

Disembodied, he could delve into in the landscapes in the deepscreens in a way that was almost 3D. It wasn't a literal seeing, like Cara's—except when he opened his eyes and looked at the video feeds—but he felt what was going on, he sensed the movements and their intentions and outcomes. On the video he saw the submarine dive deeper and deeper—trying, he thought, to dislodge the animals that teemed over it. Some of them wouldn't be able to take the deepest depths, the depths near the source, where the sub was descending so that it could fire its warhead-loaded torpedo. They couldn't hang on forever, he knew—they'd have to get into the submarine or give up. Or die if they didn't give up.

Theirs was a race against time.

Inside the sub, the camera showed him the movement of sailors in the control room—an agitation of heads and shoulders, seen from above, as some of them streamed out the door, presumably to help secure the vessel, and others stayed hunched over their consoles.

Over the ocean, and within it, the legions were fighting elementals, fighting other things. He tried to keep his mind alert in the chaos to signs of Max, but he couldn't focus enough. in the feed from the scene above the ocean, the admiral's ships, covered in darkness, were suddenly lit up by gunfire—anti-aircraft fire, he knew, maybe surface-to-air missiles, from big guns on the ships' decks that were aimed at the cloud of creatures arriving from the sky in flocks.

Only the legions' great numbers kept them coming against the gunfire, that and what Jax thought was an old-way defense of some kind, which slowed the ammunition as it approached its targets.

It didn't stop the fire, though, and people kept being hit and kept falling, the flying forms and the riders. There were bats by the thousands, Jax saw as they entered the frame in the foreground and streamed toward the ships—maybe even by the tens of thousands. There were all kinds of birds, ducks and sparrows as well as the enormous seabirds; there were swarms of big pale-green luna moths and massive beetles and wasps; he couldn't account for all that was there, but he felt their hurts. He saw the wasps cover the deck, the moths, the birds, but the sailors manning the guns were sealed off from them inside the metal cage of the ship. . . .

The ship the admiral was on, Jax knew suddenly—they needed to send all the legions there. They needed to narrow it down. His mother had said they didn't know which ship—the admiral had decoys too. But only he could revoke the order to use the nuclear weapon. If the sub itself wasn't captured, they'd have to home in on him.

You need to find the admiral, he pinged Cara. *We need to know exactly where he is.*

She had to be in the open. You couldn't let yourself feel humiliated just because you were still learning. *Own it,* her annoying swim coach would have said. Coach Essick was all about affirmations. *Own your weakness,* he liked to say, while criticizing her flip turns.

Hayley's hand on her own had made her feel better: they both had to start somewhere, and it was just their bad luck that they were stuck with taking their talents out for a test drive in the middle of a war.

But you were born when you were born; you were a kid when you were a kid. There wasn't any choosing when. You only got to choose *how*—how you faced it.

She saw the big, round table in the center of the room, where no one was sitting, no one at all. It was polished and dark. She strode up to it and stepped onto a chair and then right onto the tabletop itself; she sat down cross-legged on the cool, smooth surface and closed her eyes. Then she brought up as good a memory as she could muster of the wall of photographs from Courtney's house, the bulldog-faced man in his uniform laden with colorful medals and badges all along the chest, shaking hands with presidents and smiling a tight proud smile.

Show me the admiral, she thought, *where he is now, in his ship. I want to see which ship. And I want to see exactly where he is on it. Show me the admiral right now.*

The submarine was diving now, and some of the shallow-dwelling sea animals of the legion were beginning to let go, so he could see more of it—they were thinning out as it plunged, peeling off as it attained greater depth and the speed and water pressure overwhelmed them. Jax saw three or four deep-brown manta rays loosen their hold and float off behind the vessel, swept out of view in no time in its bubbly trail.

Jax knew what diving too deep could do to a person, and it wasn't pretty. You could lose consciousness or succumb to the intense cold or lethal pressure . . . but there was good news, too, and as he called up the knowledge he smiled: *Submarines couldn't go that deep either.*

He'd read it on some Navy blog online: *Modern nuclear attack submarines like the American* Virginia *class are esti-*

mated to have a maximum diving depth of 1,600 feet, which would imply a collapse depth of 2,400 feet. Collapse depth, or crush depth, is the depth at which a submarine's hull will cave in due to pressure. . . .

Well, sea turtles could go deeper than 1,600 feet—much deeper, down to 3,000, he thought. So could devil rays and many species of octopi and squid and . . . but suddenly there was a jerky motion on the video of the control room: a wave of motion rocked the submarine.

If he'd had an audio feed, he would have heard it; as it was he watched it to a soundtrack of silence. Among the computers and consoles, a sailor who was standing up abruptly staggered and grabbed a desk edge as he fell; another fell off his chair, arms flailing.

Something had come into contact with the sub from below, stopping its dive. Jax peered along the camera view outside, saw great hulks beneath the vessel, massive and dark but too indistinct to identify. He felt through the deep-screen for any ambient thought that could help him—and after a minute or two it came, in a wave of relief from the cephalopods that were swarming over the ship's hull.

It was sperm whales. The great beasts were lifting up the sub on their backs.

And other whales—beaked whales, he guessed. They were deep divers too.

The sub was being forced upward again.

But thinking about the depth of the black thing's dive—and thinking about the far greater depths some of the animals could dive to—Jax was suddenly struck by something else. Why hadn't his mother brought it up? The Cold's stronghold was too deep down, in the rift valley of the Mid-Atlantic Ridge: even the top of the ridge, even the very highest peak, was *far* below where the subs could go. Which meant it was also far too deep to be struck by a torpedo—before it ever got to them, any type of torpedo he could think of would have to implode under collapse pressure.

So what could the plan possibly *be*? The Cold One must have some tech that would bring the warhead deep down into his methane seep without it imploding. It wasn't impossible. If, through the admiral, he was using the massive payload of the nuke as a shortcut to climate engineering, maybe they had the means to preserve the weapon and then trigger it when the moment was right. Maybe the legions' leaders even knew about this—maybe they just hadn't bothered to inform the kids. Maybe they figured the technical impossibility of a torpedo ever hitting the gas-reservoir target under normal power was too much detail, and not something the kids needed to know about.

That idea annoyed him.

But it wasn't the *only* explanation. There were other possibilities.

The legions had overtaken the ship, but they were still on its decks, still swarming over it, searching, she guessed, for the admiral—she'd have to let Jax see, she'd have to show him so he could relay it to them. *Jax, are you watching? Are you pinging now?*

No answer.

Still, she had to keep going. Forget about that. Hold on to the vision.

Her sight swept over the ship's gray-metal body—the deck lights were blazing out into the night—and revealed sailors teeming in a panic down stairways and gangways, across the surface as loud alarms blared. The legions had landed at one end of the ship, and most of the sailors were still at the other—but a few had already met, because she saw a winged horse rear up and smash down with its hooves, she saw a huge, dignified-looking walrus moving with remarkable speed along a gangway. At the other end of the ship the sailors were piling into an armory, taking guns off the walls.

Of course they would use guns, she thought, of course—handguns, even rifles were clicking out of their brackets on the walls and being checked for ammunition, and then out poured the sailors again with their weapons drawn. . . . *The admiral,* she thought with a sense of urgency. *Show me the admiral.*

Her view swept past the huge mast laden with radar equipment past the midship structure and down and down until it was inside a shining wood-paneled room with carpets and mirrors and plush sofas. The place looked like a hotel room. At the far end, in front of a window, she saw the back of a man's head as he sat at a desk. He wore a uniform, white with gold and black epaulets—it looked like the one from the photos with famous people—and a white and dark-blue cap, so she couldn't see much of his hair. As her view moved closer in on him he swung around in his swivel chair, slowly, until he was staring right at her. As though he knew she was there!

His eyes were small and buried in his face; they were beady and fixed and had an intent look, almost accusing.

Impossible, she told herself. *He doesn't know I can see him. He can't know. Mom told me. There's no way.*

He sat there looking angry for so long she felt her heart sink . . . till he stood up and walked to a cabinet, opened it and took out a crystal bottle with a narrow neck. He poured himself a drink.

He was in no hurry at all—in fact he had the saunter of a man who was pretty relaxed. But how could he possibly be relaxed with all those others fighting and dying above? But he *was*. "Snug as a bug in a rug," Hayley's mom would have said. He'd sent the enlisted men out to fight, the sailors who weren't officers. And they were doing the fighting for him, and somehow he wasn't worried.

There was a computer in an alcove, and he leaned over and tapped some keys absently; then he looked away, almost bored, and took a sip from his glass. He strolled over to the window where his desk was, gazing out at the battle over the ocean as though nothing at all was happening.

A couple of seamen were posted at his door, she saw. They stood at attention and wore guns. The doors were closed, probably locked.

Jax! she thought. *Are you getting this?*

Jax was so preoccupied with the problem of the bomb that he almost lost his grasp on the urgent need to pinpoint the admiral's location; he snapped back to attention and could feel Cara's vision fading just as he pinged. It was dissolving from the edges and shrinking, but he scrabbled for it: faint impressions of shining wood and brass and deep carpet—and then the scene was lost. There was no blueprint, no map . . . and it was his fault, completely.

She'd tried so hard, and she'd succeeded, and he'd been distracted. He'd been too far away.

But wait: maybe there was enough for him to draw conclusions from. Maybe he could still get it. Those rich furnishings *had* to mean the admiral was in the captain's stateroom—no other cabin on board could be so luxurious, he was certain, with its velvet and paneling and polished yellow-gold fittings.

The captain's stateroom? he asked Cara, pinging.

Maybe, she thought. *He had a desk and sofas and models of ships. He had a computer and a big window. And Jax, there were two guys with guns guarding the door.*

And which ship is it—the destroyer? Or the guided-missile cruiser?

I don't know! *Which is* which?

The cruiser's bigger—about fifty feet longer. . . .

I don't know, I didn't measure *the ship, Jax! I just saw what was happening.*

Of course, I know, he pinged, *bad clue.*

He wracked his brain for a detail that might have stuck out for her; he accessed photos of the vessels in question, bringing up their names from his vast bank of data.

Wait. The cruiser has a black flag flying from it as well as the American one. A black flag with a white longhorn insignia. Like, a white set of bull's horns. Did you see a flag like that?

Yes! I saw it! I did!

He smiled fiercely to himself, proud of them both, and then winged the knowledge along, sent it streaming out to the U.S.S. *Cowpens*, to where the legions moved and fell across the ship. Gave them their target.

Six

It had made her so tired; it had made her feel weak. Too weak, she knew suddenly, to try to summon again right now—too weak to find Max and her mother. Too weak to even begin.

She sat on the table, her eyes still closed, her legs still crossed, feeling her exhaustion all the way along her limbs, not wanting to move even a bit. She thought she could get heavier and heavier and finally turn into lead, sitting here, or maybe she would just melt, like the creature that looked like Zee, into a lump of flesh. . . .

"Cara!"

Two eyes were peering at her so intently they took her back to the admiral's—how *he* had peered. Angry. Small eyes surrounded by folds of skin.

But these eyes weren't small; they were round and light blue.

"Something's not right," said Jax.

He still had dark shadows under his eyes, she noticed, and his rumpled shirt and pants looked like he'd been sleeping in them for days.

"*Nothing's* right," she said, when she found the energy to answer. "We don't know where Max is. Or Mom. And they were right there . . . with the ones who fell. . . ."

"Something else. I'm not sure the legions have . . . all the data. Either that, or Mom didn't tell us what was really going on."

"She wouldn't keep stuff from us unless there was a really good reason," said Cara slowly. "Would she?"

"First, I don't see how the Cold's plan can possibly be to have the sub fire on the rift. I called up the specs of torpedoes—I hadn't thought about it before, in all the rush—and they aren't built to reach a target as deep as the Cold's methane chambers. Long story short, any torpedo I can access specs on would implode *thousands of feet* before it got there. *Miles* before."

"You mean their plan can't work?"

"Even if it did, somehow, what about the risk of escalation? There are systems in place that monitor nuclear explosions, so an explosion like this will be noticed. Big-time. Ground Zero's near Greenland—the closest big landmass to the Cold's stronghold—which belongs to Denmark, which is part of Europe. And this weapon is being deployed from a U.S. submarine with a *Russian bomb*, and I don't know enough about the nuclear forensics but either or both sides could be blamed. There's been all this tension lately with NATO and the Russians. . . ."

Her head was spinning—as usual when Jax lectured, only worse, because she'd been so tired already.

"My point is, the Cold wouldn't want to risk setting off a nuclear exchange. He'd *never* risk nuclear winter."

"I don't even know what nuclear winter *is*."

"It's a scenario where, after nuclear weapons were used, there'd be reduced sunlight, cold weather . . . The theory is, the bombs would set off firestorms and the huge clouds of smoke and ash would bring down surface temperatures. Bad for all of us, but my point is, it'd make Planet Earth way more hostile to him than it already is. Nuclear winter would set him back *centuries*. So nuclear war is practically the only thing *both* sides don't want."

"What do *you* think's going on, then?"

"All I can think is, the ridge is a giant undersea range of active volcanoes where earthquakes register daily. Maybe the Cold needs to *disguise* this as just another quake. Make sure no one identifies it as a nuclear fission event. Then the massive methane release it triggers could look like a natural side effect of all the tectonic activity along the ridge. . . ."

"But—how's he going to do that?"

"We have to find out."

"How can we, Jax? I'm so tired. *You're* so tired."

"First we need to find out what the admiral *thinks* the plan is. I have a hunch his information might not be perfect—the Cold could be playing him. But one thing he knows well is the capabilities of his weapons, so he's gotta have more information than what Mom told *us*."

Cara had been tracing a line on the smooth table surface with one finger, exhausted. Now she looked up. She had an idea.

"Courtney," she said.

"His daughter?"

"If I can bring her here, maybe she can get him to—I don't know, maybe she can make him talk to us. Maybe she could get him to say something."

"It's not *impossible*," said Jax, but he sounded doubtful.

"Mom said anyone can use the portal system, if they just have a key. In an emergency. Without any artifacts like the windowleaf. So I could go through and get her."

"If I had a better idea I'd say don't bother. I don't think the admiral's gonna say anything to a kid. Even his own. But you know what? I don't know who the guy is. He's a wild card. And maybe it'll at least buy us some time. . . ."

"Do you know where I'd get a portal key?"

"I think the guy in the armory has all the equipment. Harris. Talk to him."

He was already turning away from her, distracted, and she scrambled off the tabletop to grab his arm.

"Jax! Wait! Once I have her, then what? What are we doing *then*?"

"First get her. Step at a time. I gotta focus now."

Alone, was all she could think, as she jogged down the dim hallway toward the armory. *Alone, alone, alone.* Once she got a portal key, if the guy named Harris even deigned to give it to her, she had to get Courtney all by herself.

And somehow, in the middle of the night, appearing out of nowhere, convince Courtney to do what she asked.

⊣⊢

He tried to stay alert for pieces of information hidden in all the lines and tangles of mindtalk—about what the *legions* knew, at least. Or what they thought they knew. He *had* to stay alert for any sign that anyone knew more than his mother had known about the Cold's strategy. . . .

But it was hard. People kept being hurt, kept being gunned down on the decks of the ships by sailors or dragged beneath the dark water by the spreading, sharp-clawed masses of the Cold's creatures. At times it was hard to separate his own thoughts from the thoughts of others, in their desperate flight—the cries of fear that struck out from below, up from the huge metal masses of the ships, up from the deep, cold waters above the submerged mountains of the ridgeline.

The cries rose and dispersed into the sky. He knew them without hearing them. And he knew the silence that they left behind.

It wasn't a normal key Harris had given her but a pattern of shadow he'd imprinted on her hand—barely visible unless you knew what to look for. He'd lifted his own hand and pressed it against hers, transferring the key—it was energy, he said, but could be passed along like a piece of language if you knew how.

He'd shown her how to move her hand in a strange little pattern when she wanted to open a portal. She figured the place where the troops had left from had to work well—she'd never seen a portal more grandiose than that one, that was for sure. So she went back to the great room and stood in a corner where, along the wall that stretched in front of her, a space had opened a few hours before to a vast expanse of the North Atlantic.

She saw nothing but wall, and though she tried to move her hand in the right pattern, nothing happened.

She tried it again. Still nothing.

She had to have it wrong.

She felt a rush of despair. It was too much—she couldn't do it by herself.

Then her arm was grabbed and squeezed so hard she almost squealed: thick, grayish fingers with long, red hair on them. She whipped her head around to see Shelley, reared up on his hind legs and inexplicably wearing a pair of ladies' glasses.

They were the cat's-eye kind, frames glittering with rhinestones, and they'd be hanging around his neck on a chain—librarian style—if the chain weren't tying the glasses onto his head.

Orangutans didn't have much of a nose.

He slid his heavy hand down her arm to take *her* hand, which he moved so that it touched the wall. Slowly, he moved her fingers into a pattern, the pinky far away from the others; he curled her hand for her, bending the fingers just so, and pressed it against the wall's surface, which was curiously warm—and not quite as still as a wall should be. A current moved beneath it, a current or a pulse. . . .

Keeping one hand on hers and shoving his other hand into his tool belt, Shelley pulled out his phone and typed with his stubby thumb:

Now see where you want to go.

She shut her eyes and saw Courtney's bedroom, trying to bring up the details. . . . There'd been a pink shag rug. There'd been those big windows with a view of the bay. There'd been a new-looking bulletin board with a couple of ribbons and postcards tacked onto it . . . .

And then the wall was gone.

Jax had been scanning the admiral's emails. He was almost sure the guy wouldn't tell Courtney anything—he never had before. He hadn't let his family in on his military activities, and he certainly wouldn't share about the terrorist ones. Now that he'd turned traitor.

And he wouldn't care much that his daughter was a potential hostage either. Jax could read between the emails' lines: the guy was pretty much a psychopath. He used people to get what he wanted.

But Courtney had knowledge of the admiral and a strong biological connection. Hypothetically, Jax might be able to use her mind as a path to her father's—history and family left tracks that were invisible to most people, but might become visible to him.

Courtney's bedside lamp was still on, so Cara didn't have to step into a dark room. That was good, because her last memory of sneaking into a stranger's bedroom at night wasn't a good one (reflexively she glanced at the long white scar on the side of her finger).

She felt like the interloper she was as she stepped through the space onto the softness of the pink shag rug. To firm up her resolve she reminded herself of Jax waiting in front of his monitor, of her mother and Max out somewhere in the bitter chill of that far-north night. She thought of the human-sized bird on the white bed in the hospital wing, its huge eyes closed forever. Still hesitating, she looked back at the view through the portal: a rectangle of otherness, suspended in the middle of Courtney's large bedroom. Within the rectangle was the cavernous room of the library, its domed cathedral ceiling.

Shelley had disappeared again, and the vast dark room had only a few amber sconces burning on the walls. Other than that it looked empty.

Cara took a deep breath and turned back to Courtney.

"Courtney? Wake up. It's Cara."

Courtney made a grumbling noise and turned over, so Cara had to reach out and shake her lightly on the shoulder.

"I'm sorry, but it's Cara. Wake up, OK? I need you to come with me."

Another couple of seconds and Courtney turned over again, her eyes wide open this time.

Cara had no idea what to tell her. They stared at each other, Courtney rubbing her eyes and sitting up.

"I'm—I'm sorry to be here uninvited like this," Cara stuttered. "But I need you to come with me."

Courtney, still half-asleep, threw back her covers and got up, her hair tangled and falling over her face. She wore white flannel pajamas with bunches of red cherries on them. Cara grabbed her hand.

"Come on. We need your help. I'm really sorry, but I don't have time to explain. We have to hurry."

And she pulled her gently toward the portal.

"Weird dream," murmured Courtney, but even though she thought it was a dream she reached up and slid something out of her mouth: a retainer. She placed it neatly in a plastic box on her bedside table and turned back to Cara, and they stepped through the opening in the air.

⁂

He was glad his videofeeds didn't show him actual battle scenes; it was bad enough sensing the victims' pain. He didn't envy Cara her gift of summoning—not now. Not with *this* to see.

When he'd been a hollow, he'd been down in the ocean near the ridge and had seen a great machine scraping the bottom—the Cold getting rid of his enemies, trawling the depths to kill off the marine animals that weren't allied with him. There were whole fleets, he knew, devoted to this—fishing fleets whose nets were deployed for the Cold, claiming as "bycatch" all the creatures they killed that weren't going to be sold as food. Meanwhile the Cold's great machines scraped the bottom, pulling all manner of beings into their mesh. Mammals and sea turtles alike were cut by the unbreakable lines or suffocated because they couldn't get to the surface to breathe.

"Jax," came his sister's voice. He handed off his communications lines to the next station, then opened his eyes and turned away from the monitor.

Cara was standing there with a girl he'd never seen before, except in a snapshot on his mother's screen—Courtney. She wore pajamas and had a confused kind of smile.

"She thinks she's dreaming," whispered Cara.

"It's wild," echoed Courtney. "We went through a hole in my room. In my room's *air*."

"Then welcome to the dream," said Jax.

Bring me the females, interrupted a voice in his head.

Disturbing, until he saw the great ape eyeballing him.

Shelley rolled back his seat at the end of the row and curled an index finger, beckoning them over. Jax went and the girls followed, Courtney tottering like a sleepwalker in her colorful flannels and striped, fuzzy toe socks.

It was a good thing she thought she was dreaming, Cara thought, or she'd be mortified.

But they had bigger concerns: as large as life, on Shelley's monitor screen, was a pale, belligerent, bulldoggish face.

The admiral didn't look happy.

"*Dad*," mumbled Courtney. But she still spoke dreamily, not too worked up about anything. "Why's your head on the computer? I didn't know you Skyped." She turned to Cara. "I didn't know he Skyped."

"Who's there? Give me a visual!" growled the admiral, and Cara realized it wasn't like Skype, in fact, because he couldn't see them. He was still in his captain's cabin, but somehow Shelley had patched through to his computer in there. They were looking at him through its camera.

"They still haven't gotten to him? The legions?" she whispered into Jax's ear.

Shh. He has an audio feed, Jax said into her mind. *They've found him—they're outside his door, but he's basically barricaded in.*

So her vision *had* helped. She'd *done* something.

She felt a spur of pride, until she remembered Max and her mother could be . . .

And pushed that away.

"Is that my daughter? What the hell? *Courtney?*"

Cara squeezed Courtney's shoulder softly. She might get scared, if she suddenly started to doubt the dream scenario. No, she *would* get scared. Of course she would.

"Whoever you are, you're late to the game," went on the admiral sharply. He sounded so sure of himself that no one else could affect him. "It's already in motion. The sequence has already been triggered. So whatever blackmail you think you're doing, you won't get results."

"What sequence?" asked Courtney curiously.

Suddenly Jax turned from the monitor and took hold of Courtney's hand.

"Please," he said softly, "just reach out to the screen here, it's going to feel a little odd," and he guided her hand toward the deepscreen image.

As Courtney's fingers touched the screen they sank in, and the admiral's bulldog face rippled.

"Tell her what your objective is," said Jax, fast and low, as the admiral's face jerked back away from Courtney's fingers. But not fast enough—somehow the fingers had brushed against it, Cara thought. And at the same time she saw the strong current in the air from Jax to Courtney, the current of mindreading that only appeared when he was deep into it, far deeper than his invisible, casual pings. . . .

But then it was Jax who jerked back, out of contact with Courtney, just as she pulled her hand back too. She gazed at the tips of the fingers as she wiggled them.

"That felt ticklish," she murmured, and at the same time—

"No!" burst out Jax.

Shelley leaned forward and hit a key on his keyboard and the frame around the admiral widened to show more of his stateroom, the other people standing behind him. A couple of guys in military uniforms, all blocky-looking, geared up and loaded down with equipment—and then another, younger guy in front of them, not wearing a uniform at all. Like them, he was holding something blocky and black that hung on a strap slung over his shoulder. A gun.

It was Max.

And he was smiling.

"This one yours?" asked the admiral.

Jax felt a flash of rage like a burn on his face. Cara had cried "Max!"—she couldn't help herself—and that was enough to tip off the admiral.

"He's ours now," said the admiral.

It had worked, thought Jax, he'd pinged through, but now he was panicking: *They have Max.* Why the smile? It wasn't fake, he was sure. Max's smile was proud, almost arrogant.

How? How could it be?

"But Jax," whispered Cara. "It's not *really* Max, is it? It's probably one of those shapeshifters—those anomalous— whatever. Is that what it is?"

It's him, he pinged. *Don't say any more. The admiral may be able to hear us, even when you whisper.*

"I have a hostage myself, I guess," said the admiral. "So we'll be signing off now. We have to be going, before your friends bumble their way in here."

Why would Max be with them?

The admiral reached up to cut off the uplink, but somehow Shelley wouldn't let him, hunkered down over his keyboard, typing fast with his large fingers. He made a grunting sound as he pinged Jax: *We'll let him think he cut us out, but we'll keep an eye on him.* The blur of the admiral's hand hovered in the foreground, then dropped away.

He turned his back on the screen, receding into the crowd of sailors, into whose ranks Max had also faded. All they could see now was an indistinguishable crowd whose bodies, moving to and fro, filled the frame in faceless blurs of movement.

"Wait. There's another way out?" asked Cara.

Jax peered in close, trying to penetrate the deepscreen: maybe they'd finally see some of the Cold's transport tech, whatever he had that was the counterpart of the old-way portals. He moved his Burners through space using fire, the Pouring Man using water—but how would he move *people?*

Could it hurt Max? Change him?

They still had audio: a barrage of automatic weapons fire from multiple guns—so loud and unrelenting coming out of the deepscreen that no one could hear anything else. Rat-tat-tat, again and again, a roar almost like people screaming.

And maybe they *were* screaming, thought Jax, just yelling as they fired.

Then all at once the crowd of bodies thinned out until there were spaces between them again. A few seconds later Jax and the others were looking at a gaping hole where the large cabin window had been.

And a room completely empty of people.

They just shot their way out the window.

It was Shelley, pinging.

So much for the quality of American manufacturing.

"They just—left?" asked Cara, dumbfounded.

"Yep. Gone," said Jax.

"Is it time to go back to bed?" mumbled Courtney.

"I don't *understand!*" cried Cara. "What was Max *doing* there?"

"I have a theory about that," said Jax slowly. "And I got a glimpse into the admiral's head too. Just for a split-second, when I was touching Courtney and she was touching *him*, but I think I know what he's planning."

"How'd you stick my fingers through that the computer screen?" asked Courtney, playing with a button on her pajamas. "It felt like warm water. Except it stung a tiny bit. Water that stung—"

"I'm sorry for that," said Jax. "It's not what they're built for. Typically only the mind can go in. But I broke you through for a split-second. We're desperate for information here."

"I mean it stung a little but it was kind of cool . . ." said Courtney, nodding distractedly. She'd moved on from the button to a strand of her hair, which she was twirling around a finger as she stared at Shelley. He'd switched out his old-lady glasses for what appeared to be a biker's helmet. "Is that a gorilla?"

Shelley heard, apparently, and made a spitty raspberry with his lips.

"Oh," said Courtney, drawing back. "Gross. This is the bad part of the dream."

"I want to take her home," said Cara to Jax, low. "I feel bad for her."

"Let's head to the library," said Jax. "And I'll tell you what I know."

He didn't *have* to tell the ape. The ape had already read him; the ape already knew.

⚞⚟

As the three of them walked down the hall toward the library, Courtney dawdled behind the others to admire the art on the walls (touching it sometimes with one poking finger, as though to see if it was real). Jax told Cara what he'd learned from the admiral.

"I didn't see what he thinks of the Cold—that was too buried. I only got his knowledge of the Cold's immediate plans. Cara, he's going to use the submarine *itself* as a weapon. He's going to aim it deep into the rift with the nuke inside."

"But won't it get crushed? You said it couldn't go that deep."

"It *has* to get crushed. And the nuke will be set to go off when it does. He's planning to sacrifice all the guys in there. Which I'm pretty sure they don't know. But the admiral knows. He knows and he's going along with it."

"But how can he—I don't get it."

"The plan is to send it down so that just as the sub pops out in the rift, near a fissure that goes particularly deep, it'll implode, crushed by pressure. The bomb will go off, and my guess is, it'll be deep enough by then that no one will know it was a nuke. The military folks will count the sub lost at sea, and the earthquakes the bomb sets off up and down the rift will expose hundreds of methane seeps. If not thousands. All that stuff's going to spew out in a massive rush."

"But he can't use a portal to get it down there, can he? Portals are *our* tech . . . I didn't think he could use it. Right?"

"He can force others to use it for him. Maybe he's always had double agents we don't know about. Either that, or he has new . . . prisoners of war. Hostages. Or traitors."

They looked at each other over Courtney's head.

In the library people stood around a long table, watching maps that glowed and turned in midair. It was a pretty cool-looking display, if you weren't used to holographs, but Courtney wasn't paying attention.

"Max," she said. "Is it Max in *Where the Wild Things Are*? 'Cause I've dreamed about him before. Max and his sailboat, remember? I loved that book when I was little. . . ."

"No, this Max is our older brother," said Jax.

Cara shook her head, still trying to figure out how Max could be so crucial. And why or how he could possibly have turned against them.

"I mean, Max doesn't have a portal key," she protested. "He doesn't know anything *about* it."

"He can probably access one," said Jax. "The keys are a form of thought energy, plus the muscle knowledge of how to 'turn' them with your hand. They can be learned or given, but if you're given one they don't last long. Max . . . Max has a highly unusual talent. He hasn't told anyone yet. He wouldn't have told me if I hadn't stumbled across an email—but he can get into people's heads. It's a kind of extreme empathy. You become part of another person's mind. He'd only ever done it with Zee . . . and what it looks like to me—and I only know this from what the admiral was thinking—is that Max, when he was shot down—"

"Wait, he was shot down? But he looked fine!"

"—he had to have been shot down over the ship, otherwise . . . and then he must have been turned. Somehow the empath thing went wrong. I don't know more yet."

Cara's right hand was tingling, she realized. When she lifted it she saw the shadow-handprint was still there—but was it fainter? Could it be?

"Is it fading?" asked Jax.

"I don't know—Harris didn't tell me about a time limit. But it is starting to feel different."

"They don't last long at first," said Jax. "You kind of—borrowed it. It's like a temporary license."

"Well, I should take Courtney home. . . ."

"No," said Jax, and shook his head. "There's something we need more than taking her back. Especially now that Max has defected. Some*one*. We need Cub."

"Cub? What can *he* do?" she asked, exasperated. She wanted to get Courtney safe in her own bed. She felt guilty for deceiving her and dragging her around half asleep.

"He can hack," said Jax. "And feed me data. Courtney? Umm, go lie down. This can be the end of your dream, OK? You were a big help. Go back to sleep."

Obediently Courtney shuffled toward a long, antique couch against a wall; obediently she lay down, her head on a tasseled cushion, and brought her knees up so she was curled and ready to sleep. Cara was startled.

"How did you make her—"

"I know this wasn't what Mom told us to do, but she isn't here—and I haven't studied any more of the prophesy we relied on last summer either, because it's in an old language and I haven't translated it yet. So get ready to turn your hand when I ping you a scene of Cub's room."

A bit grudgingly she did as he asked. Into her mind came a picture of a boy's bedroom she'd never been in, with posters of outer space on the walls and sci-fi planets with multiple moons. From the ceiling hung a mobile with planets orbiting the sun—and there was Cub, sleeping in a small bed apparently left over from early childhood since it was shaped like a rocket. Occupying a table beside his desk was the biggest model she'd ever seen of a spaceship, marked U.S.S. *Enterprise NCC-1701*.

When she opened her eyes again the scene hovered in front of her through the fuzzy, faintly shining edges of the opening.

Jax didn't bother to step through himself. Instead he just yelled.

"Cub! Wake up!"

It worked, too. His geeky best friend sat straight up in his narrow bed.

"Come through the portal, Cub. There's not much time and I need you. Oh! And grab your laptop."

Cub picked up his glasses from the headstand. He had something on his nose that looked like a Band-Aid and covered a large stripe of his face.

"Snore strip," explained Jax.

You had to hand it to Cub, though, he'd gone to sleep in his clothes, which, while slobby, was convenient. And once he had his computer in hand he didn't hesitate for a second. Just stepped right through.

All those movies and TV shows had obviously prepared him.

Seven

Cub would be able to help with data gathering, Jax was sure—
but if he was being honest, he needed Cub here just because
Cub was his friend. But the moment Cub came through, Jax
realized there was another person whose help they needed
even more—for Max. To bring Max back. The person Max
felt he owed a debt to, a person he believed he'd abandoned.

She's so sad, he'd said to Jax, and when he said it he'd
looked pained.

Cara's portal key was almost gone, and he hadn't assimilated the knowledge himself yet, so they depended on it. . . .
She wouldn't like this. It was dangerous. But he had to do it.

So he grabbed her hand again while Cub was still looking around in wonder, his eyes large and owlish behind his
glasses, saying, "What the heck *is* this, please? What was
that portal thing? Can I get an expla*nation*?" and before
Cara could object he'd pressed her hand back against the
wall and pinged deep into her mind his best, most detailed
memory of Zee's house, where she lived with her fisherman
single dad. The portal yawned open, not to her bedroom
but to the small, messy living room. He pinged *Wait here!* to
Cara and Cub and jumped through.

He raced up the stairs and opened one door after
another, knowing the portal key was flickering in and out

on the surface of Cara's hand. That had to be Zee's dad, asleep. The next door was hers—but her bed was empty.

So he raced down the stairs again, beginning to panic a bit, but there was a light being shed from a doorway near the back—the kitchen. Here she was, standing in front of the open refrigerator, just staring in. She wore a T-shirt and sweatpants and flip-flops, and it was true—somehow she did look sadder than she used to, and thinner too.

Come on, he pinged her, because he didn't have time to waste, and as he'd done when he told Courtney to go to sleep he exerted a small compulsion so she couldn't say no easily. He'd rather not, but he had to. He grabbed her hand and pulled her after him, and she couldn't resist, and they got back to the living room to see the portal shrinking, with Cara and Cub yelling from the other side. "Jax! You've got to come back! Right now! Jax!"

He wasn't worried—not about this—because Sabin or one of the others would bring him back, but he didn't want to divert them from their tasks and he wanted to do this himself. So he boosted Zee ahead of him through the portal—now the size of a small window.

"What the hell?" roared a deep voice. "Kid! What the hell's going on here?"

Jax whirled to see Zee's father standing in the middle of the living room, wearing boxer shorts—and holding a small handgun. He wasn't exactly pointing it at Jax, though.

"I'll bring her back soon," he promised.

Zee's father shook his head, confused. "You're—aren't you Max's little—"

Jax turned, sensing the portal was going to wink out any moment, and leapt headfirst after Zee.

He felt his stomach being scraped and then he crunched his head on Cara's knee. *Crack across the frontal bone,* he thought. He liked to know what part of him he was breaking. When he picked himself up off the rug he realized his skull would be fine; it was his middle that hurt. He raised his shirt to check the skin beneath it. The stripe looked like a mild electrical burn, he thought, a red welt across his midsection like a belt.

"Jax!" said Cara. "What were you thinking? *Zee?* And what *is* that?"

"A minor burn, I think," he said. "But I had to bring her, Cara. We need her. To get Max."

They all stood there staring at each other a little dazedly: Jax, rubbing his head; Cara, looking at Zee with alarm; Zee, like a deer in the headlights, her eyes wide and astonished; and Cub, clutching his laptop under one arm and still wearing the snore strip pasted across his nose.

"Might wanna take that off," mumbled Jax, and gestured at it.

Cub muttered something and peeled off the strip.

"You need to tell me what that *was*," said Zee. "What just *happened* to me? 'Cause the way it looked was, I jumped through some kind of a wormhole deal with Max's baby brother pushing me. Am I on drugs?"

187

"Not a *wormhole* as such," corrected Cub, shaking his head quite severely. "Officially, the Einstein-Rosen bridge is a hypothetical topological feature of spacetime—"

"Hey, Cub? We don't have time for that right now," said Cara.

"You came into my house in the middle of the night," said Zee to Jax firmly, "while I was raiding the fridge. I never even heard the front door open. And then you dragged me through a hole in the air. Before I know once and for all that I'm a mental case, you need to tell me what's going on. We clear?"

Jax had to hand it to her: she wasn't that fazed.

"It was a portal we opened," he said. "There's a—I don't know how much you know, Zee, but remember last summer, when you helped us by lending us kayaks one night? All this is related. And Max has been avoiding you because he had to, because we believe you're being used, probably without your knowledge or consent, by—"

"Aliens," interrupted Cub. "Jax thinks it's aliens. Bona fide extraterrestrials. I say no way. I say it's purely a home planet bad guy, trying to terraform the Earth so he can live on the surface. But none of them listen to m—"

"Listen, Zee," said Jax. "Listen carefully. You're safe in here, at least, safe from being used by this guy. We call him the Cold. There are safeguards in here called wards, and they lock him out unless he breaks them down, which this time I don't think he will. But out there in the real world, outside these walls, well, there he *can* use you. Or at least, that's what we believe. So we don't know if we can trust you, in general. That's why Max had to back off. But Max is in danger now—*he's* the one being used—and we need you to help me try to get him back. And make him safe again."

Zee was quiet for a moment, her brow knitted.

"I don't know what you're talking about, some bad guy using me," she said finally. "But I do know Max has been a total jerk to me for, like, the whole year. So I'm not sure why I owe him *anything*."

She looked Jax straight in the eyes.

"Or you."

"I'm telling you—"

"You have some weird way of explaining. You pull me from my—into this—and you expect me to—"

There was only one fast way to make her understand, and even though he'd made a deal with Cara and Cub not to do it, he felt he needed to now.

So he pinged Zee with a compressed version of the whole story, and he watched her step back physically. She stood there for a long moment processing.

"How'd you do that?" she asked, finally.

"I have abilities," he shrugged. "We all do. In our family."

She looked at them both, then shook her head quickly, making her decision.

"I'm in," she said. "But Max better kiss my feet for this."

"Then let's go," said Jax.

"Go where?" asked Cara.

"If we get Max out of the admiral's clutches, we may also be able to stop the sub from getting into the rift valley. *Maybe.* But I don't think we can do it through consoles and monitors. I know Mom didn't want it, but we have to go there ourselves. We have to go where the fight is."

⸻

Cara trusted Jax's instincts more than anyone else's, true, but this was far-fetched. If the Cold's whole plan for world destruction hinged on a skater kid named Max from Wellfleet—well, he wasn't much of an evil genius, was he? And anyway, no one could have known for sure that Max would be available to brainwash. . . .

But Jax had dispatched her to the hospital wing to get Hayley without explaining any further. They might well need Hayley's healing skills where they were going.

Hay a healer, Cara thought. Wow. She'd never have called that one in a million years, and she was pretty sure Hayley herself wouldn't have either. But hey, maybe now she'd grow up to be a doctor. Instead of, as she'd written on her middle school career-counseling form, CELEBUTARD.

In the infirmary, hovering midair and seemingly held aloft in a cradle of hundreds of threads of light, was a whale.

It might have been small for a whale, but it was huge for the room. A sperm whale, she thought, because it had the big, square forehead that only sperm whales had. That blocky head was pointed right toward her, too, like the front of an oncoming bus—so big. So square. So gray.

It reminded her of the famous blue whale model, almost a hundred feet long, suspended from the ceiling at the Natural History Museum in New York. She'd seen it on vacation one summer.

But this one was real.

"An infant this young can't have developed skills yet, mindtalk-wise," said one of the healers surrounding the whale with her hands streaming light. "Biggest brain in the world, but he can't tell us what's hurting or broken. Looks like there's some hemorrhaging over here. . . ."

Sabin, Hayley, and some others stood beside a bed at the end. Cara drew near, hesitating to interrupt—it made her nervous to be around injured people—and saw past Hayley's shoulder to the creature lying with closed eyes on the bed. It looked like a human-sized squirrel, except it had wings: it must be a flying squirrel, or something similar. Like the human-sized bird she'd seen before, it was still as it lay there, and the sight gave Cara a sinking feeling.

But she'd come to get Hayley, and she couldn't turn away. Her eyes were fixed on the creature as she reached out to tap her friend on the shoulder. Its middle was covered in an odd, translucent bandage, and this bandage, instead of covering everything like regular bandages, let you see the wound if you peered in close. Beneath it was—a mass of red and brown.

Then she did close her eyes. See-through Band-Aids: *that* was a mixed blessing.

Hayley was startled at the touch on her shoulder.

"Sorry—we need Hayley to come with us," Cara said to Mr. Sabin, across the bed. He was looking at Cara sympathetically, which confused her. Then he turned back to look at the flying-squirrel face and Cara did the same—the face really was still. Its big, shuttered eyes had long lashes on them. Like a Barbie or something, Cara thought. And it was covered in seaweed, its rubbery pods, strings, and leaves. Poor creature. "Is this guy—will he be OK?" she asked, keeping her voice quiet.

"She," corrected Mr. S. gently.

And then the face and body were changing, subtly and quietly, until it wasn't a six-foot-tall squirrel on the white cot at all.

"Mom?" she said. Her voice came out gravelly.

"We're doing everything we can," said Mr. S. "Why don't you take a minute. And then leave her to us, and you and Hayley can go."

The others around the bed backed off till she was the only one standing at the bedside anymore, except for Mr. Sabin, who hovered in the background.

"Um. Can she hear me?"

"We induced a coma, so it's not impossible. But really we can't know," he said. "With comas like this we don't ping. She needs peace and quiet. But you can talk to her if you like. It might help her—you never know. I'll be just over here, OK? If you need me."

She looked down at her mother's familiar face, with its elegant bones and clear skin, its few faint lines around the eyes. The seawater had left brine and weed tendrils around her neck and in her hair that hadn't been washed off yet. Was she in pain now? Could you feel pain if you were in a coma? But maybe. . . . She thought of asking Mr. Sabin.

Once she would have just broken down, she thought. But now—her mother would want her to go help Max. And the rest of them. Her mother wouldn't want her staying here.

Love wasn't just watching. Love was doing something.

"I have to go," she whispered. "Mom, listen. I'm going to do my best."

Then she reached out and kissed her mother's warm cheek quickly; she grabbed her hand and squeezed it before setting it back gently on the silky fabric that covered the cot. She turned and was going to call Hayley when she saw her already waiting, just standing waiting patiently at the door.

She couldn't put her finger on what was so weird about that until a couple of minutes later, as they were walking at a fast clip back to the cathedral. Yeah, that was it: that was the first time she'd *ever* seen Hayley standing and waiting while doing absolutely nothing—not texting, not talking on her phone, not playing a handheld game, not browsing Best and Worst Dressed Celebrities lists, not trolling for free music. Not holding her phone at all. Just waiting, watching, and listening. As time passed.

Cara reached out and grabbed Hayley's hand. Two hands held in as many minutes. Sappy. But it didn't feel that way.

Before she turned to go she gazed a moment more at the face of the whale. She could only see one of its eyes, but the eye was open. It looked so intelligent and at the same time so alarmed: it had a gentle curve above it and one below it that reminded her of eyebrows, and the eye itself had white on either side of the iris. Just like a human eye.

They needed their own shapeshifters, their own flying and swimming machines. He could navigate based on his recall of the battlefield, as long as Cara was there to feed him information on Max's location by using her sight. And Cub would back him up from home base: Jax proposed to use nothing more than the humble cell phone for contact with him, betting the military ships would have their own arrays of dishes the signal could bounce off of. And he'd get the portal-key tech from Harris.

Zee, who was now sitting on a library table a few feet away and swinging her legs, waiting, was the biggest X factor. They needed to take her with them—getting through to Max might turn out to be critical—but once she'd left this warded building, she was vulnerable. He didn't know if he could learn to defend her fast enough, not with everything else he had to do.

He sensed Cara was upset about something, but he didn't want to ping her unless he had to; it was a slippery slope. When he'd convinced Courtney to sleep on the couch, when he put a small but hard suggestion in Zee's mind compelling her to come with him, those had been baby steps toward—well, toward being a person he didn't want to be.

It was dangerous, doing things that gave you control over people. Even getting a glimpse of that kind of power could corrode you. His mother had been teaching him that. The hardest part of having power was knowing when *not* to use it.

"So how—how are we doing this?" asked Cara, coming up with Hayley beside her.

"We need a shifter," he said. "Or shifters. I'm working on it. Cub, can you help me? You're going to work off your laptop and a deepscreen while we're out in the field. Zee, stick with Cub and mo, please. Cara, Hayley, you guys want to take a catnap for fifteen minutes? I know we're all really tired. . . ."

He glanced down at his phone: 4:22 a.m.

Cara looked past him to the couch, where Courtney was sleeping.

"We'll leave her here," said Jax. "I'll ping the teachers and let them know who she is. She'll be safe."

He left the two of them settling onto sofas near Courtney's—the library was dotted with them, along with deep old musty-smelling armchairs—and motored through the maze of halls with Cub and Zee following.

"What's the plan, Stan?" said Cub. His voice sounded even more nasal than usual.

"You really are a nerd, aren't you," said Zee. But her tone was friendly.

"Free range," answered Cub. "Wild roaming."

"That's beautiful," said Zee.

"Zee's going to ride with me," said Jax. "You'll be safe here, Cub, but I need you to stay close to your cell the whole time. You'll have an overview of the battlefield through the monitor I'm going to show you, and you'll have your own laptop for research backup when I ask you for it. The main thing you'll be doing is just watching us through the deepscreen and answering whatever questions I shoot you."

"And you're gonna be doing what?" asked Cub.

"We'll be flying, but we may have to hit the water too. I'm working on it."

They were coming into the screen room, where all the same people were still hunkered down working—except for Shelley, who'd gone elsewhere.

"So you're going to get Max back?" asked Cub, as Jax sat him down at the station that had been his (meanwhile staring at the fluttering moths two consoles down). "Uh . . . do you know where he is?"

"Right now he's a moving target. Cara will help me with the locations, but I'll need your help on that as well. I'll need you to help locate him on the map when I send you the description of his position—this one here." And he leaned over the monitor. "See?"

When he pulled up the image of the area, with its video feeds in the corners, Cub's mouth hung open.

"What the hell," he said. "What kind of OS *is* this?"

"Old," said Jax. "It's a really old OS . . . combined with a new one."

Leaning close, Cub reached out and touched the screen exactly the way Jax had seen Cara do it. His fingers brushed against the silky surface.

"It *is* permeable," said Jax, "but only when it's told to be. It's a communications interface, not for transportation."

"Wow," breathed Cub. "I've never seen anything that looks this 3D. Except for, you know. Life."

"It's cool," admitted Zee, standing behind them with her arms crossed over her chest. "And you don't even need the plastic glasses."

By the time they left Cub at the monitor he was deeply engrossed in trying to figure out its workings, though he'd promised to be on duty as soon as Jax dialed him in.

"I have to figure out how to defend you," Jax told Zee as she walked beside him on their way to the armory. The armory door slid open as soon as it sensed him and Zee standing there—slid open to reveal a room lined with so much tech he'd never seen before that it thrilled him. There were organic things, suits made out of living materials that rippled in their transparent containers; there were machines, only a few of which he'd come across in all his time browsing the archives. One looked like a recorder or flute that he recognized from a training manual as sonic and sublethal; another looked like a crossbow. In the middle of the floor stood a teacher he vaguely recognized from his first trip to Thrace, a time when he'd been barely conscious. It must be Harris.

Yep. Harris, came the ping. *In wartime, we don't ask for permission. What do you need, Jackson?*

It was a relief not to have to speak.

I need a lot of things.

She was dog-tired, but she couldn't sleep a wink. Hayley sure could; her face looked angelic with its wings of blond hair and peaches-and-cream skin. But her snore wasn't that heavenly. She should have borrowed Cub's snorestrip, Cara thought.

Courtney and Hayley were sleeping like babies, while she could barely close her eyes without feeling pressured to open them again.

Her mind was racing: her mother's face waxen, black seaweed curling on her neck. Max, smiling and holding a chunky black gun. The unseen bomb, encased in a submarine that silently cruised the ocean, full of sailors who didn't know they were about to die. *Don't think past today, right now,* she told herself. No use thinking into the future. That was part of her mission of practicality. She couldn't let her imagination run away with her. . . . From a dark corner of the library something caught her eye, and she raised herself up from the couch cushions on her elbows.

It was the cat they'd seen before that walked on its hind legs—a Japanese cat spirit, Mrs. O had called it. Cara forgot its name. The cat stood with its forearms hanging limply; it was gazing into a screen Cara couldn't see. Behind it, a cloud of moths fluttered—also focused on the screen. A battle scene, probably. They were watching what happened.

And as the standing cat watched the screen and Cara watched the cat, she heard a strange, sad sound. Like someone crying, but more musical. A song, she realized, a song that was terribly sad.

She felt tears streaming down her face. She couldn't help it: the cat spirit's song was so beautiful and so sad.

It wasn't till she was distracted by a loud scratching and clucking that she turned away and wiped the tears off her cheeks.

Admittedly, when he asked Harris for shifters for them to ride, he'd pictured something majestic. Something that'd look noble if this were a movie. Flying horses, maybe. Or the beautiful, dappled-gray hippogriff from *Harry Potter*. He'd needed top-notch shapeshifter people, he told Harris, smart and experienced ones he wouldn't have to *explain* everything to, ones he could ping easily with instructions or who could just read his mind as they flew and do the work for him.

As he and Zee stepped back into the main room he had a rude shock, because here they were—the only available flying beasts. They must be the dregs of the shifter army. Not dragon-like raptors, not graceful seabirds, not even the flying squirrel form his mother favored that could leap hundreds of yards on its powerful wingflaps.

Nope. What they got wasn't any of those. What they got was giant chickens.

Well, hens, technically, he guessed, since one made a joke right away by laying a huge egg on the library's Persian-looking rug. The others laughed hysterically at that and laid their own eggs. (Which was to say, they clucked and made high screeching tones he was pretty sure indicated laughter.) He wondered what their human forms were; he tried to ping the biggest one to find out more about them, but all he got was a sharp reprimand. She didn't like it.

I'll read you whenever I need to, boy, she pinged back. *You can ping me too, but stay outta my personal business.*

Each monster hen stood larger than a horse and had different coloring, though all five of them had matching lavender-white feathers on the tops of their heads. Harris had even equipped them with small platform seats you'd have to call saddles, plus collars around their feathery necks with grips, Jax saw, to grab onto . . . could chickens even fly? Admittedly these weren't as fat and round as regular barnyard chickens—they were scrawny, almost, and more muscular looking. Well, they had to be good fliers, or Harris wouldn't have given them to him. Harris was proud of his armory and his duty to it.

Wait, thought Jax. Why so *many*? He'd only requisitioned four. But there were five of them strutting around, five giant, clucking, smelly chickens whose idea of hilarity was laying dinosaur-sized eggs on the carpet. . . .

And that was when he saw Shelley. The orangutan, wearing a weird garment that Jax suspected was a ladies' fur coat, was already loping up to the biggest hen; he jumped onto its back without warning, causing it to screech indignantly and stagger under his weight. As it righted itself, wings thrashing, one giant talon clumsily crushed one of the massive eggs. Yolk leaked out in a wide radius.

"*Shee-yit*," it squawked out, and the other hens half collapsed in another laughing fit.

It smells bad up here, pinged Shelley. *Like week-old KFC.*

"Enough of this," said Jax, quite loudly. Suddenly he felt annoyed with the monster hens. This was serious. This was life or death.

They fell silent instantly, surprising him. He noticed Cara was at his side, with Hayley yawning behind her.

He didn't need to ping Shelley to conclude the ape had decided—he was coming with them.

"We're as ready as we're going to be," Jax said softly to Cara, while Zee was busy climbing onto her monster. (It kneeled oddly.) "Zee's defended from the Cold for now, but her defense will only hold as long as I'm conscious. So if anything happens to me, you probably need to get away from her just in case. Her shifter knows the deal—they all do. And I have the tech to open portals now. As soon as we're through, I'm going to need you to envision Max's location. You're the best source we have for that. I'll ping you freely during the rest of this, Cara. I have to. And Cara? Hayley? You don't have to steer. Just hold on and trust me till I send you an instruction."

"Hi, chicken lady," said Hayley, patting the head of one. "Thanks for being our ride. That's pretty cool of you."

The monster hen inclined her head graciously.

As Cara and Hayley were getting on—scrabbling until they figured out where the handholds were on the collars that were half buried in feathers—Jax jogged over to touch the wall and open the portal; the scene spread out beside him as he ran back to her and clambered up. It was lighter than he'd expected, he realized; dawn was finally breaking in the sky above the ocean.

That was good.

"What if I plummet to my death?" asked Hayley as they waited for Jax to adjust his cell phone in his pocket and stick his earbuds in his ears. "No offense, chicken lady, but I'm not used to the whole riding-a-bird thing. One time I rode a dinosaur named Q, though."

Was it Cara's imagination, or did her hen and Hayley's put their heads closer together, dipping their beaks oddly, when Hayley said that? Hens' eyes didn't show a ton of depth—even these huge ones. She couldn't tell when the hen-monsters were looking at each other, due to only one eye being on each side of their head instead of both in front, like with people.

But the hen-monster eyes were kind of extraordinary, orange-gold and surrounded by bright-red skin. The black pupils were very small and precise within the golden iris, and the eyeballs flickered around beadily. . . .

She glanced away to face the vista looming in front of them: the first leaks of sunrise over the ocean. The water was dark still, but on the horizon the light of a sun they couldn't yet see was turning the bottom of the black night sky deep blue. And beneath what looked to be a faint cloud sat the small armada of ships.

The cloud hanging over those ships—she knew it wasn't a raincloud. It was a midair fight.

Atop his hen-monster, Shelley was restless. He gestured *come on* with his hairy hand and made an impatient hooting sound.

"I know. It's time," said Jax. "You all ready? Cara, focus and find me Max. And chickens—let's fly."

They squawked in a disgruntled way. But then they ducked briefly down, bounced up and took off, flapping their wings powerfully. Cara had to admit it wasn't bad— it was easier than riding Q had been. Where her legs hung down from the seat, the monster hen's massive body felt strong, and not as light-boned as real birds were. A deep thrill ran through Cara and made her feel determined as they rose and sailed into the portal, a rush of chilled air hitting her almost as hard as the smell of the sea.

And then they were aloft and soaring over the middle of the Atlantic.

What she wanted to do most was look around, but she couldn't, not yet. Without her they didn't even have a destination here. So she gripped her hen's collar and closed her eyes. *Max, Max, Max,* she thought. She'd grown to love the feeling of it already—open to everything and everyone, as though she could be them. As though she had no borders.

The sight came rushing in faster than ever, dizzying. Beneath the seat she felt the solid body of the hen—the hen's body was reassuring, she realized—but here was Max, though the scene spun before it settled.

A long black island lay in the water—no, not an island. The submarine. It was slickly wet all over, and had a big thing sticking out the top—like a black tower, wedge-shaped and mean-looking, with a flat piece across it that made it look like the tail of a jet. As she watched, a hatch like a manhole cover in the top of the turret opened and out climbed a couple of men in uniforms and orange lifejack-ets, who stood there holding guns. They were looking away from her, off the other side of the tower—at a puffy gray motorboat that was skimming its way over the waves. The boat slowed and a line was thrown to one of the seamen; then three people stepped from the boat onto the top of the submarine.

The first was someone Cara had never seen before. The second was Roger, a coworker of her mother's at the ocean research center. Roger had spied on their mother for years, all the time working for the Cold while he pretended to be her friend.

And the third one was Max.

Back in the powerboat, she saw someone stand up, someone wearing bling on his uniform and a cap with a brim and gold trim: the admiral. He threw Roger a grin and then saluted him jauntily as the boat began to motor away again.

This meant, of course, that Max was going to be aboard the sub—the sub whose mission was to implode.

Jax, are you getting this?

I'm getting it, he pinged back. The ping had a touch of grimness. *We just need to know how to get to the sub from here, the shortest course. Cub can give us a heading from the living map on the deepscreen. He has a God View.*

She watched, feeling helpless, as Max followed the other two down the hatch and into the black, hidden bowels of the ship. *How can we follow it, Jax?* she asked, her eyes still closed, the chill wind in her face. *If it goes under?*

We could, but it wouldn't do as much good. We have to board it before it dives, he pinged back. *There's tech on the camera that's stuck to its hull. Both GPS and old way. And now Cub's figured out how to access audio from their control room, where we have another video feed—I didn't know we had audio—and he just has to figure out how long till it dives and the best path to get us there.*

This was why kids had no place being in a war in the first place, even a secret war like this. They could get—hurt. Max had screwed up somehow; he'd been vulnerable, and now he could get killed. And they could too.

We're not just kids, thought Jax. *We're people with something to save that's beyond us. We're people with skills that can make a difference. Don't let it overwhelm you, Car. If you despair, they've already won. You're doing great. Did you ever think you could master the sight so quickly? You were struggling. But look at you now. Look at what you've already summoned.*

Thanks for the pep talk, Jax.

But she was worried about Max. She was worried about her mother. She was worried for all of them, and it made her stomach tight.

OK. It's ten minutes till it dives. So that's how long we've got to get there. Well, five, because it'll take us time to get in without being seen. . . .

It sounded impossible.

She felt her hen-monster banking to the left, instinctively tightened her grip on the collar as her body leaned sideways, and finally opened her eyes.

She'd never in her life had a more magnificent view. The other hen-monsters flew in formation, the five of them in a V-shape with Jax and his hen at the front tip. With their wings spread out, the hens looked almost graceful. Almost. She caught Hayley's eye, beside her—Shelley and Zee were off to Jax's left—and Hayley smiled. Then she looked down. The ocean was spread out beneath them, the sky above, and she was in the middle of it: part of the sky, part of the air.

It's amazing, she thought. *I'm so scared for Max. And Mom. And us, even. But still. This is the most alive I've ever felt. The most I've felt at all. Flying!*

And while we fly, thought Jax, *let me show you something. Let me give you a vision. For a change. It's something I learned. About us, about Mom.*

Jax would have to know by now that their mother was in the infirmary—after all this pinging.

I did get that from you, he pinged. *But this isn't that. This is about our people. Close your eyes again so you're not distracted.*

She did. And something faded into view: a grand and beautiful landscape. Green fields of long grass bending in the wind as herds of odd beasts ran through them, blue rivers running free through deep valleys cut into towering mountains.

We never learned this in school. This is something most people have never known. But now I do, and you should too.

It was tens of thousands of years ago. *This was the promised land for us then,* said Jax. *Earth was heaven for us. . . .*

And she saw people living in caves and huts in the beautiful place, and other people, standing on a ridgeline overlooking their settlement.

The people we were at first are now called the Neanderthals, said Jax gently. *That's us, looking down. In the valley beneath are primitive homo sapiens some call the Cro-Magnon. This is our first contact. We were a more advanced culture, with ways that seemed like magic to those who didn't know them. We were peaceful, but not abundant. We sought safety in numbers: we joined with them and had children. We brought them our art, new kinds of thinking, even some aspects of language. We kept our old-ways talents and nurtured them privately, but we also assimilated. And for many years, for many generations, we lived together. Thousands of years.*

But there were some of us that didn't choose to join with them, fearing their warlike nature. Those old people took other forms. The forms of sea turtles. The forms of mammals in the sea. Mammals on land, as well. Other primates. Some of us shapeshifted in perpetuity and joined with other animal groups, and grew apart from us, living within their own cultures. Ananda is descended from some of these. And still others remained their own people, apart, peaceful but less hardy, and eventually those "pure" Neanderthals died out. There were wars between them and our ancestors, sadly. We tried to stop those wars, but too much aggression was latent in our Cro-Magnon families.

I won't show you the wars. Today I want you to see the beautiful parts. What I'm telling you is, we are the remnants of the hybrid people, Cara.

We are the last vestige of the Neanderthals.

Eight

He'd shown her as fast as he could, and there was so much more to tell, but they were homing in now on the sub's position.

The monster hens knew their next form—he could feel the body of his hen softening beneath him as she prepared to change—and Shelley, over to his left, was pinging him that they needed to go faster, faster, faster. (Shelley's monster was pretty irritated with him; Jax felt her pinging back Shelley in a cranky mode.) It was the other kids he was worried about, how they would cope with the morph and stay calm underwater. How freaked out they'd be. He needed to warn them what they were in for, but he didn't want to scare them—it was a tall order.

They'd have to clamber up onto the sub and down that open hatch without being seen by the seamen who were patrolling topside—hard. Really dicey.

He pinged the others. *The hens are about to shift into a water form. Hold tight to the collars and hold your breath at the beginning while they pull up the tech for your bubbles. Got it? We're going to dive. You'll have just a minute underwater—as we pull up to the sub, we have to find a way to get up on top of it. Don't let go of the collars till then. The air you'll be breathing is attached to the saddles, so stay locked in.*

The monster hens were pulling up short now, coming in for their water landing—they wouldn't be able to paddle much, thought Jax, not having webbed feet. But it would be a fast shift. He hoped.

Cara didn't know what to think about Jax's crazy story about Neanderthals, but she didn't have much chance to dwell on it, because her hen-monster was flapping its wings to land, and the motion shifted its body so that she almost slid backward into the tail feathers.

She did what Jax had told them to and held tight to the collar; her feet were dipping in the water now, and a wall of seawater splashed over her head and shoulders. She was cold and she was wet, floating on the surface for a few dis-orienting seconds as the hen moved in a flurry beneath her. And then the creature was lengthening and its feathers were shrinking back into their holes; its back was turning gray and leathery, sprouting fins. When it raised its head for a few seconds she saw it had a very long, flattened snout with teeth along it, sticking out of the front of it like a chainsaw. The snout must have been three feet long.

Now they're in sawfish form, pinged Jax. *Sawfish are named because of that thing you see sticking out at the front—a rostrum that looks exactly like a saw. It's actually an extended nose. These guys can get to be twenty-five feet long and weigh five thousand pounds, but they're almost blind and don't love cold water. The real ones, that aren't just shapeshifted, are nearly extinct. But these ladies are tough.*

She was still seated in her boxy little saddle, which reminded her of a tiny booster seat Jax had used to sit at the table as a baby—but now her legs hung down farther, on either side of the sawfish's narrow, shark-like body. The giant fish had wings like a ray, only not as wide, and she inched up and bent her legs so that she could perch toward the back of where those wing-flaps were—she wanted to feel secure but not interfere with their movement. Behind her were a set of pretty big dorsal fins. The collar, which she was clinging to with a vicelike grip, didn't look comfortable at all for the fish form: the sawfish had no neck.

Next to her Hayley, who was more flexible, was practically doing the splits on her own beast, seated right on top of the wings. Cara hoped she didn't fall off.

Then the water was rippling over the strange creatures' heads and rising around them as they went under—she took a gasping breath just before her head was submerged. Her eyes squeezed closed against the saltwater as she felt the shock of freezing cold.

But then there was warm air around her and she opened her eyes. It was hard to see beyond her and the fish, but she knew she sat in a bubble of air around the saddle; she was moving so quickly there were dense streams of smaller bubbles around her.

Hold tight, said Jax. *Just a few more seconds. . . .*

Her body was shivering, her lower legs and feet getting numb . . . and up there, ahead, were men with guns.

Shelley was a good climber, he bragged. *I'll kick your ass,* was specifically what he pinged. *Kick your ass at climbing. Kick your ass into the middle of next week.*

What's your point, Shell, thought Jax. He hoped the sigh came through.

They were almost there.

I'll be the vanguard. You're just shrimps. I'm strong, also. Kick your ass at fighting.

OK, so what are you—

These colors don't run. Asshole.

Jax had no idea how they were going to get past the guards.

Me, said Shelley. *I'll take them both on. You pups hold tight.*

Jax saw a great dark bulk in the water ahead. It was huge—he hadn't understood how huge until now—yawning everywhere in front of them, black, and a heat came off it, and a deep, rhythmic throbbing. Even without knowing what he knew, he'd find it ominous. It was a war machine.

He turned his head and saw Cara and Hayley on his right, on his left Zee and then Shelley—who was clambering off his saddle.

Jax had never seen a great ape swim—the long, hairy arms looked like they were windmilling. Then Shelley was right up against the vast blackness ahead of them, moving along it, only his torso and legs visible beneath the water-line—soon even his reddish back and bulky toolbelt disappeared, and last his legs and dangling, long-toed feet. Shelley's toes looked a lot more like fingers.

A wet, bedraggled orangutan vs. at least two men with big guns.

Jax didn't feel good about it. In fact, all of a sudden he felt an urgent pull to follow. Shelley could be badly hurt—but how could Jax climb up with no ladder?

His sawfish-hen pinged him then. She could jump, if she shifted again. But they'd attract tons of attention. There'd be no cover up there.

Shift anyway, he said. It would distract the guards from Shelley. *Shift, please. Now.*

I gotta help Shelley, he pinged Cara. *Stay put unless I tell you not to.*

But—

The saw-like protrusion shrank away: there was a rounder head, with whiskers. She was a seal. She dove down to get momentum, Jax clinging desperately, then swam in a swift circle—up again, and then they were leaping, leaping into the air, and ahead of them was the black island of the sub, and they crashed onto it.

Jax rolled off, bumping his head, feeling bruised all over, but the seal just lay there, motionless. She'd hit the metal bulk harder than he had, he knew, and had his weight on top of her . . . he was wondering if she was hurt, but he also had to find Shelley and the soldiers—there couldn't be much time left till the dive.

But he couldn't see them. Ahead was the looming tower that had the hatch in it. He picked himself up and ran awkwardly along the sub's metal skin, soaking and cold and slipping on its surface, his sneakers squelching. When he got to the tower he slowed down and crept around it—and sure enough, on the other side there was Shelley, hunkered down with his fists dragging.

And looking right at him were the two uniformed men with guns.

But instead of pointing the guns, they were gawking, half-smiling at him, their eyes practically bugging out of their heads with amazement.

"How the hell did that thing get here? They can *swim*?"

"Crap! What's that around its waist?"

"I dunno. Some kind of weird diaper?"

"Is it a gorilla?"

"Naw, man. That's a baboon."

BABOON? pinged Shelley, thundering in Jax's mind. HOW DARE YOU?

He hunkered down and then turned his face up at them, doing a cute/goofy act that looked ridiculous to Jax, now that he knew the guy. Then he ambled over clownishly. Uh-oh.

Jax pinged him. *Don't try it*, he said. *Don't try to attack th—*

But Shelley ignored him and lunged, reaching one long arm up to the sailor on his right and grabbing at his weapon, which he struck sharply out of the man's hand. It clattered onto the metal. The sailor was caught off-guard, but his companion quickly raised his own gun, the smile abruptly dying on his face.

You don't want to hurt the ape, Jax pinged the seaman, and clamped down hard on any resistance. *You'd never hurt this cute little ape. You want to drop the gun. The ape's just playing. Must have escaped from a container ship. Zoo-bound. Let's take it home as a pet.*

It made his head ache to compel the man, but he had no other choice.

Drop the gun. Do it.

And finally the sailor did. Jax couldn't release him, even though it was hurting his head more and more, a screaming pain in the temples, but he had to control him from this moment forward or they were done.

As Shelley scrambled to pick up the guns, Jax was already tiring. Mind control at this strength was vicious. It felt like the concussion he'd got from falling off a swingset once.

You're going to go swimming now, both of you, he directed. He had to get them away from him. *You're going to swim toward the U.S.S.* Cowpens *over there, and you're going to make it. It's going to be killer. You're going to set a new Navy record. Take your boots off first. And then just swim.*

Shelley stood fumbling clumsily with the guns, making Jax nervous, as the two sailors started pulling off their boots slowly. Jax wanted to tell the others to come up, Cara and Hayley and Zee, but he had to focus—and just as the seamen dove off the boat he heard loud thwacks behind him, combined with short shrieks of alarm. The seals had brought up the others.

Here come the laydeez, pinged Shelley. *What time'd your geek friend say the dive was happening?*

Jax slipped his cell phone, in its see-through drybag, from his pocket and read the last update from Cub.

T minus one minute, he pinged. *Let's get them in. We have to close the hatch for the dive.*

Jax spun around to check that the seamen were swimming toward the cruiser on the horizon—and they were, with long, heavy strokes. He thought of his seal, lying unmoving. The hard crash of her body against the ship's metal. He turned to run back around the tower that was blocking his view. Shelley, meanwhile, scampered up the ladder at warp speed and disappeared.

The sub was shaking now, throbbing faster, Jax thought, as he came around the tower and saw the three girls standing there, dripping, a little stunned-looking.

"Come on!" he yelled, "up there! Get in!" though he was aware the crew, down in the bowels of the sub, had to be watching them. They had their periscopes. It was guaranteed: once inside, they'd find a firing squad waiting for them. He had to strategize on that—but where were the seals?

We shifted, came a faint ping. *We're in mole forms.*

Worry later, he told himself, *they're grown-ups, they can take care of themselves,* and then he and Cara and Hayley and Zee were all banging across the top of the sub and climbing the ladder, where Shelley squatted waiting at the open hatch.

As they climbed in he heard the sound of commands over the submarine's intercom—commands he didn't quite get since he hadn't studied military jargon. Shelley closed the hatch. Jax wondered why the admiral had directed the sub to keep to its dive schedule, given that its captain and crew must have seen the seamen striking out across the water, and given they knew the kids were here.

As to the seamen, he answered himself, sure: the admiral didn't care. And as to the kids being aboard, likely he didn't think they were a credible threat.

And maybe they weren't, if they were about to be captured.

Use a portal, pinged one of the moles from wherever they were hidden. *Right now. From here. Your brother's in the Crew's Mess. That's where we need to go. It's in the Operations Compartment, and there are too many people between us and them to go on foot from here. They're armed and ready to take us into custody.*

How do you know?

Dear, we know everything.

So while they hung there on the ladder rungs—the muffled sounds of running below, some orders being shouted—he pulled up the tech for portals and described one in the air.

Just jump, he pinged Cara and the others. *Jump now.*

It was awkward to turn away from the handholds of the ladder and then launch yourself into nothing. For a second she was paralyzed by fear. There was still empty space below, and if she fell—but she had to leap and she did, landing on all fours on a rubbery mat that scraped her hands and knees.

In the pocket of her soaking windbreaker, the shifters squeaked. She hoped she hadn't squished one.

A-OK here, A-OK here, they pinged.

Around her were men with guns. More of them.

"Ow!" she yelled as Hayley slammed into her and then Zee fell in on both of them. Jax and Shelley somehow landed on their feet. As they scrambled to rise she heard a number of rapid clicks—*Yeah. That's the gun safeties*, Jax pinged. *Just act like you're behaving. I've got this.*

She rose. So did Hayley and Zee, grunting a little at the pain of landing.

"Put your guns down, Shelley," said Jax aloud, and raised his hands in surrender. She and Hayley and Zee followed suit.

Shelley, she saw, was holding two guns just like the sailors', one in each hand. He looked like a guy in an action movie. Except for being an ape.

"I don't care if you don't want to," said Jax firmly. "Do it. We're outgunned, see?"

Shelley raspberried. But then he reluctantly set the guns down on the floor .

"And now," said Jax, turning to the ring of sailors, "for you."

Right away there was a stream of current from his head, one she recognized from before: he was pinging them, but it was one of the deep and forceful pings he hardly ever did. The stream twisted and rippled and then spread out over them, blurring her view of their faces and making it look like the faces themselves were being stretched and distorted.

She didn't know what Jax was telling them, but after a minute they, too, dropped their guns. They stood stock-still and blank-faced, bewildered. As though they didn't know how to feel. Or what they were doing.

How had he done it? Had he won them over?

"Collect them," said Jax to Shelley. But his voice was strained. She looked down and saw his small hands were clenched into fists and shaking.

She wished she could protect him. But she didn't know what was happening. The men were turning to each other, all of them in pairs, fiddling with their hands. Some put their hands behind their backs while others slipped hand-cuffs on them, a plastic kind she'd seen on TV that looked like twist-ties; then the half that was already handcuffed, bringing cuffs out of their palms, struggled to put them on the others. All this took place in silence, and the second cuffing went on and on painfully as the men fumbled with their bound hands. She watched Shelley gather the guns and pile them in a corner . . . and then, glancing over at Jax, she saw something on his neck and stepped closer. There was a trickle of blood running out of his ear.

"Jax. You're *bleeding*," she whispered.

He swiped at the drip but didn't pay much attention, so it just smeared.

As the sailors sat down on the floor, cuffed and cross-legged, she could see what had been hidden behind them: Max and Roger. They stood at the end of a long table—and they were both smiling. It was weird, but their smiles were exactly the same—as though Max was some kind of replica of Roger. In some way, she realized, his face *wasn't his own* because it was a mirror of Roger's.

Max held his gun, cradled like a baby, but Roger held nothing. He looked relaxed and casual.

"Welcome," said Roger. "Nice, Jax. We don't need the little toy soldiers anyway, do we? They just get in the way."

The stream coming from Jax faded, and as it did the sailors broke their silence and started angrily muttering— they didn't like being tied up. Not surprising.

"You know this is a suicide mission," said Jax.

"For some," said Roger. "Not for me."

"How do you figure," said Jax flatly.

"I'll be leaving."

How long did they have? Cara wondered. The sub was diving deeper every minute. Which meant every minute brought them closer to being too deep—closer to going through a portal yet to be opened. And closer to crush depth.

She didn't like it in here. It felt stuffy. She hated that there weren't windows.

Max was staring at Zee.

"Max," she said. "I came to get you. What's wrong? Why are you doing this?"

Max's face looked stiff, almost wary, but he didn't take his eyes off her.

"Max, I know what happened. I know you blew me off because of—all this. And I forgive you."

Max's smile held for a long time. Cara felt her stomach drop. It wasn't doing any good.

But then, in the space of a second, his expression changed. The smile wavered and fell; his posture changed and he stepped away from Roger. Jax, she saw, looked pleased as Zee crossed over to Max, as she looked down at the gun and then pushed it gently back. He let her; she threw her arms around him and after a second he put his around her, mumbling something that sounded to Cara like *I thought I was him.*

Roger was watching with curiosity.

Curiosity, Cara saw, but not anxiety. Roger wasn't worried in the least by Max's defection.

"It's nice that you brought her here for him," said Roger to Jax and her, condescending. "They can go out in style. She's no more use to us anyway. After you made her, in the house with the old lady, we let her go as a sleeper—her cover was blown. She's nothing special at all."

Max and Zee were ignoring him, talking to each other in low, inaudible tones.

"So now who's going to open your portal for you?" Jax asked Roger.

"Your brother here was bait, that's all," said Roger pleasantly. "For such a genius, Jackson, you're a really dumb kid. So brilliant and yet so stupid."

"There's no way I'd ever do it for you," said Jax. "None of us will."

But he looked nervous now, as well as shaky.

"No. The Cold has his own tech for this. And yes, he'll make it look like seismic activity. Meanwhile, you and I are leaving together," said Roger. "I'm going to take you to your real family."

"I'd never come with you," said Jax.

"Of course you will," said Roger and came around the end of the table. "You belong with the Cold. With our side. It's where you've always belonged. You don't know who your biological father is at all, do you?"

Cara reached out and grabbed Jax's arm. It was rigid.

"How do you think you came by that neat trick you just used? The mind control? Think, Jax. *That's* not an old way, is it? You have so many of them. But you also have other skills, don't you. And those others . . . they come from your father's side. The control comes from the Cold. Just like you do. You have a lot of him in you. It's time to leave these petty dissenters behind. Join the real power. Your father needs you, Jax. It's the moment to find out who you really are. Leave them. They're nothing compared to you."

This is some Darth Vader bullshit, pinged someone forcefully. Who?

Shelley. It was Shelley.

I don't know if we can save the crew, Jax pinged a little hysterically.

Don't listen to him, Jax, thought Cara.

But he's right, pinged Jax. *That I have the Cold in me. I see it now. I read it from Roger. More than he's saying out loud. . . . I know where I came from now.*

Let's just get out of here. Please, Jax. Let's go.

"He doesn't need any old-ways tech to get the sub to its target," said Roger. He was close to Jax now, looking down at him. It was weird, Cara thought; he seemed kind of fatherly even though what he was saying was warped and had an edge of bitterness. "He can do that by his lonesome. So your little adventure was all for nothing. You can't stop this, but we're so glad you thought you could. We relied on your childish delusions of power to get you here. But they don't *have* to be delusions, if you learn from him. You can be his rightful heir, Jax. If you choose to be."

The blood was dripping faster from Jax's ear.

"Take us out, Jax. Come with me. Let's pay your father a visit."

Jax. Forget about the sub. You heard what he said—we can't stop it. Please, Jax. Just get us out of here. Please, Jax, just take us home.

There were almost 150 crew aboard, according to the info Cub had sent him. The people in this room were just a small part of them. And they were regular people. They were just enlisted guys, doing what they were told. A few officers too, but he was pretty sure they were in the dark. They didn't know about the target, they didn't know the nuke was going to be used—and they definitely didn't know what the future held for them.

The very near future.

Roger was trying to manipulate him in an obvious way he wasn't stupid enough to fall for, even with his head throbbing so hard he could barely think through the pain of it. The Cold should never have chosen a guy like Roger to speak for him.

But then, the Cold had never been much of a people person. Had he.

And Roger was right: it *was* time to pay him a visit.

A creaking, rumbling noise was coming from overhead. Or maybe from the walls around them—Cara couldn't tell. It made her tense up in fear.

"Oh no," muttered one of the cuffed sailors to the one next to him. "No no no. We're approaching crush depth!"

"Give me a vision of the control room," said Jax to Cara through gritted teeth. On the collar of his coat the blood from his ear had started to soak in. "Control room, now. Please."

So she squeezed her eyes shut and took a while. Finally there it was, a room with computers and things that hung down from the ceiling. Full of men—and one woman, she saw.

"Got it," said Jax, and when she opened her eyes again he was moving his hands oddly in the air. After a minute the groaning in the walls subsided.

"Phew. We're climbing again," said the sailor. Sweat was pouring down his face.

"Wait. Did *he* do that? The kid?" asked the guy next to him.

I've got to get us nearer the surface before we land, pinged Jax. *Hold tight.*

"*Stop it,*" said Roger harshly, and grabbed at Jax, but Jax fell away, sitting down hard on the rubber mat, and at the same time one of the sailors rose and tackled Roger, knocking him down too. Then another sailor was on top of him and they were both wrestling to hold Roger pinned. Had Jax done that? Or had they acted for themselves?

The sub shook a bit. She didn't like that either—it wasn't much better than the groaning and rumbling.

"What's happening?" cried Hayley.

Cara grabbed a table edge to steady herself. The shaking got harder and harder. She was holding her breath.

"Too fast!" shouted a sailor. "Too fast!"

And then there was a crash. Alarms went off, shrieking.

"We've got to get topside," yelled one of the sailors to Jax. "We're taking on water. There's got to be a breach!"

Jax nodded, exhausted, and suddenly the sailors were free. Cara felt it as Jax loosed his hold on them, and they rushed for the door, their hands still cuffed, piling out in a hurry. . . .

"What's happening?" repeated Hayley.

"Go. Go with them," whispered Jax.

"Not without you," said Cara, fierce.

"Give me a hand, would you?"

She helped him up, relieved—for a second she'd thought he had some other plan, that he intended to go with Roger.

Then they were running along a hall, following the sailors, Shelley loping behind. Jax could run, but only slowly. Out of the corner of her eye she saw Shelley reach out and stick his big, hairy hands on Jax's back, maybe holding him up or pushing him forward.

And when they climbed the ladder and stepped out the hatch she saw the sub was beached—it lay sideways along a small, rocky island with nothing on it but a tall, metal tower, right in the middle. All around the island was water, as far as the eye could see.

As soon as they'd clambered down off the sub, jumping onto the rocks—sailors teemed around them, shouting something about "containment" and "security" and talking on devices attached to their shoulders—Jax collapsed. He lay on a flat boulder.

I need some time, he pinged weakly.

"Whatever you're doing that's making your ears bleed— stop it," said Cara urgently. "*Please.*"

I did stop. I let the men go. We have a screen around us, so they'll ignore us now. But that's all I can do for the moment. . . . Took everything I had to bring up the vessel. It hurts.

Zee and Max were still clinging to each other, looking around, confused, but Hayley knelt beside Jax.

"Here," she said. "Jax. Let me see."

Cara was distracted by a stream of angry words as Roger was wrestled out of the hatch, two sailors holding on to him. But their hands were still cuffed together, and Roger, who wasn't cuffed, pulled himself out of their grip easily.

One fell back and hit his head; it made a crunch against the ship. Shelley, standing beside Jax, let out a roar of anger and fast as lightning jumped back onto the top of the sub, where he tackled Roger. They fell with a thud.

Shelley sat on Roger's flattened back like he was a pony. Then he reached out and pulled Roger's hair.

Roger squealed.

"Wow," said Max. It seemed like forever since he'd spoken. "That's one mean monkey."

Shelley held up one hand at him. Middle finger raised.

"Ape," corrected Zee. "*Great* ape."

Cara turned and looked down at Jax. Hayley had the light coming from her hands, bathing Jax's head.

"What's she doing?" asked Max.

"I guess she's trying to heal him," said Cara. She was a little in awe: Hayley could bring the light.

"But I need to know what's wrong," said Hayley, looking up. "This is—this is only pain relief. The problem is, I don't have diagnostic skills yet. Making the pain less is easy, but for healing—I don't know what to focus on."

Looking at Jax's white face, his eyes closed and sunken, Cara had an idea—a weird one, she knew, and far-fetched, but an idea all the same.

"Let me see," she said. She tried to bring up Jax's head—as though she was scanning it. *Let me see what's wrong*, she asked. *In his brain. Show me.*

And there was a picture of a brain, lit up with tiny lines. And around one of them was a blur.

"I think maybe something is burst," she said quickly to Hayley, when it faded. "Or blocked. I mean, I see all these little lines—and then one has a kind of blot on it."

"A blood vessel, I bet," said Hayley. "That's good. I mean not good, but we did that back at Thrace. We did one of those already. Cara! Did you see where?"

"Around—here, I think?" And Cara touched Jax's head, his silky blond hair. It was warm, and she realized how cold her hands were—her whole body, the clothes still wet, was shivering in the chill ocean air. . . . If the picture had been from the same angle as Jax was, in space, then the problem was on the right side, near the top, but she didn't know more than that. "I can't be more exact. I'm sorry."

More sailors were pouring out of the hatch, talking and yelling to each other, streaming around Shelley and Roger like they weren't there. Like no orangutan in a tool belt was seated atop a facedown guy in fatigues on their beached submarine.

Jax's mental screen—of course.

Jax moaned as Hayley moved the light around. She was using both hands, right near the right side of his head, biting her lips, Cara noticed. What if she messed it up? She was even newer at this than Cara was at visions . . . and what if Cara had just seen something normal in there? What if she was wrong? It was his *brain*. Her baby brother's impossible, genius *brain*. Should Cara tell her to stop? Should she tell her just to stop the pain, so Jax could open a portal and take them back to the Institute? And be healed there?

She was torn. There was no one to ask. It couldn't be Jax—he was beyond questions.

"Are you sure this is a good idea?" asked Max. Like *he* was a mindreader.

"I'm not sure," said Cara. "I'm not sure at all. . . ."

"I can do this," said Hayley. "I've done it before. Trust me."

"But if what I saw was *wrong*—"

"It has to be now," said Hayley. "There's no time. Just—be quiet, OK? Give me some space."

Cara stepped away, reluctant. She remembered asking Hayley the same thing: to give her peace and quiet while she tried to summon—

Hey! squeaked a small voice. Pinging. *Get us the hell outta here. We had to rest after the last shift, but now we're done resting. And short on oxygen.*

Plus the lint in here is disgusting. Our noses are sensitive.

So she unzipped it. Five mouse-like animals squirmed out. They jumped onto her arm, small, sharp claws digging in so painfully she let out a squeak of her own. They were brown and furry but with weird pink snouts that looked like opened-up flowers.

"What the—" said Max.

"Oh right! It's the mice that used to be chickens!" said Zee, as Cara bent over and stretched her scratched arm out onto a rock. They scampered down the arm and stood on their hind legs, paws in front of them.

"I'm lost here," said Max. "Chicken-wise."

Let her try, came a ping. *Let her try to heal him. And by the way, we're moles, not mice. Juvenile star-nosed moles. Don't you even watch* Animal Planet?

"So. What do we do now?" asked Max, looking at Cara.

Your baby brother got the sub off target. Excellent work. Now. I am going to communicate with the legions for next steps.

The mole must have been pinging all of them then, because Max looked baffled and then said, "Communicating with the legions? Long-distance mindtalk? From moles?"

But the moles were growing and shifting in a blur of color and movement. Bigger and bigger. It was like watching Claymation, Cara thought, at high speed.

And then they were five old ladies, bundled up in floral parkas. One of them had bluish-gray hair that sat on her head like a curly helmet. She looked cranky—and also vaguely familiar, but Cara couldn't pin it down.

"That tall metal thing right beside you happens to be a cell tower, smartass," said the cranky lady with the blue hair, squinting at Max through her thick glasses. "So. Who's got a phone?"

"Um—Jax's is in his drybag," said Cara. "Wait. I'll get it."

She stooped beside Jax, who was lying very still as Hayley cradled his head with her rippling light, and rummaged in his coat, pulled out the bag with the cell in it. Handed it over.

"Well, lookit," said the blue-haired lady. "Five bars. The wonders of military technology."

She strolled away from them, phone to her ear. The other ladies talked together in a huddle.

More and more sailors were climbing out of the hatch and massing on the rocks, so many it was a crowd. They were jabbering about a hull breach—but the nukes were secure, one said, as Cara edged near and tried to make out their words. The reactors were stable.

"Search and rescue time," said a woman sailor near Cara, while gazing right over her head as though she weren't there. "Bring on the spiked hot chocolate, please."

"Cara, wait. She's calling—who?" asked Max. "Old shapeshifter lady command central?"

"She's calling your mother, kid," said another old lady, looking over her shoulder from the huddle. "We're all tapped out as beasts of burden. Did you want to spend the rest of your life here?"

It wasn't long before they looked up and saw helicopters in the sky. But not normal helicopters—long, thick-bodied ones with rotaries on the tops of both ends. The sailors cheered as they grew near.

"So—but those are for them," said Max. "For the crew. Are they going to take us with them? They don't even see we're here!"

He turned to the nearest sailor and yelled full-blast, waving his arms.

"Hey! You!"

The sailor, a tall guy with bushy eyebrows, didn't blink. He gazed right through Max and picked his nose.

"Nice," said Max, and shook his head, defeated. "Maybe it's time for Jax to get rid of that screen."

But Jax wasn't able to do anything. He lay as still as ever, and Cara flashed back to the other time. Before, they hadn't been able to bring him back with the light tech, Cara recalled, and felt a chill.

But he'd been a hollow then. Not injured like this.

This was different.

"Be patient, Max," said the cranky old lady, coming back to them and handing over Jax's phone. Cara slid it into the drybag again, then into the pocket where the moles had slept.

"At least she knows my name. Before it was just Smartass," grumped Max to Zee.

"We have a private flight coming," said the lady to all of them. "These chumps are flying economy. I'm Trudy, by the way."

"I know where I've seen you," said Cara suddenly. "In the hair salon!"

"Yes, I admit it. I get my hair done," said Trudy. "Guilty."

Cara looked past her to the other ladies. Now that she'd made the connection, she recognized a couple more of them. One of them had her white hair in a short, boyish cut, and Cara had seen her at the salon as well—she remembered because Hayley had watched her pay once and whispered, *She never tips. Not even a buck. Cheapskate!*

So the old ladies were locals. Huh.

At the other end of the rocky island the first helicopter was landing, its loudness only partly muffled by the wind.

Sailors organized themselves into neat lines to get in, some of them carrying duffel bags, some carrying nothing. When the first helicopter took off, the second landed, and then the third, and finally a fourth—and last. That one only had a few sailors in it; they could have easily fit in too . . . but no. Cara watched it take off toward the west, its chop-chop-chop slowly fading. She hugged her coat around her. At least it was drier now. The one benefit of the wind.

They were alone in the middle of the Atlantic. Five kids, five old ladies, one obnoxious orangutan, and Roger.

She glanced at the top of the abandoned submarine. Roger was sitting up, his hands and feet cuffed together. Shelley patrolled behind him, loping back and forth, holding one of the sailor's guns. He must have snatched one of their hats, too, because he was wearing a goofy-looking black beret.

"Cara?" she heard, faint behind her. "Max?"

Jax.

He was sitting up.

Nine

Everyone crowded around, congratulating first Hayley and then him—they'd both done way more than anyone would have guessed they could. Even Shelley scrambled down off the ship to run over and bare his teeth at Jax in what was supposed to approximate a human smile. (Not an orangutan thing: typically the baring of their teeth wasn't a good sign, Jax pinged her absentmindedly at the sight of the ape's yellowy choppers. Of course, Shelley wasn't pure orang: he had plenty of the old blood in him.)

They were still clustered there, asking Jax questions he mostly shook his head at and said were for later, when their own ride hove into view on the horizon, and they watched it approach in excited relief: a small red helicopter. When it got near enough to descend, Cara could see two people inside.

A pilot. And their mother.

She stepped out onto the rocks and they ran to greet her, hugging her—"Whoa, whoa, I'm still not a hundred percent," she said when Shelley tried to get a rough hug in.

Presently they all stepped back to ask what was going on.

"The real Navy's on its way," she said, beaming. "The ones higher up who aren't in on this. They're coming to secure it now, take charge of the rogue weapons. Along with some friends from NATO coming in from the east. And that's down to you—you, Jax, and all of you kids. You did this. I couldn't be more proud of each and every one of you."

"*I* didn't do anything," said Max, his head hanging. "Worse *than* nothing. I got used as bait. When I tried to use my—well. A so-called talent. After they shot you down beside me I kind of flipped and I tried to—but I couldn't control it. And then I was someone else who turned out to be near. Someone I really didn't want to be." He nodded toward Roger, a small figure now hunched on top of the sub.

"It was a group effort," said their mother "And you being used as bait . . . that was on me. That was *my fault* for not briefing Jax fully, not telling him the Cold had his own tech for bringing the sub down deep."

"But if I hadn't tried to—"

"We'll get your talent working for you instead of against you, Max. You need training, that's all. It's a tremendous gift. It'll be a privilege someday, I promise."

"But what about the—what about the enemy?" asked Cara. "Where's the admiral?"

"He's in our hands now. The legions got him when he returned to his ship. He'll be taken into military custody."

She walked past them toward the sub, and they followed.

"Well, old friend," she said to Roger. "Looks like you've fallen on hard times."

When he looked up his face was red and twisted in rage. Cara was afraid, despite the cuffs that were binding him.

"This round may go to you," he said. "But it's far from over. Just ask your kid. The prodigy. He knows."

Roger was right, of course. It wasn't over. Not until the Cold was finished and done with.

But he couldn't think that far ahead.

He knew what he had to do.

I'm going to face him, he pinged his mother privately. *I have to. And you have to let me. This is the way it has to be.*

Never, pinged his mother back. *No, Jax. You're not ready. Maybe one day, but not now.*

I don't have a choice.

"My son's not going to him," she said to Roger, aloud. "Kids, all of you. Into the chopper, please."

The old ladies were shifting again—this time into gull-like birds. Not big enough to carry anyone, but still big.

"We'll take the high road," said Trudy. "We don't hold with high-tech flight."

And just like that they took a running start, flapped their wings, and flew off westward.

Max and Zee looked at Cara, who nodded, and then obeyed, holding hands as they jumped from rock to rock toward the waiting helicopter.

"Come on, Cara," said Hayley. "I'm freezing!"

"Go on," said her mother firmly. "Jax and I are having a quick word. Then we'll join you."

Jax watched as the girls walked toward the chopper, Cara turning to look at him over her shoulder. The look was pleading.

Go, he pinged. *She's right—you need to go.*

You too, she thought back at him. *Come on, Jax. Please. Don't listen to Roger.*

It's not him I'm listening to.

Then don't listen to the Cold!

The one I'm listening to is me.

She turned away after a moment and climbed up into the helicopter, her shoulders drooping.

"I'm dead serious, Jax," said his mother, grabbing both of his hands in her own. They were warm. Her face was so earnest, so full of love, that it almost hurt him.

"He's my biological father, isn't he," he said.

Her expression changed a bit, sadness behind it.

"He is," she said softly. "You were rescued from him. Your biological mother is one of us—a dear, dear friend. One of the very best of us. She thought she could change him. She made a heroic effort. She was willing to give up everything for the chance to turn him into something good. But in the end she failed, and we had to rescue both of you, back then. You're not—you see, you're not the age you think you are. It's one of the reasons you're so advanced, with your talents. You had another form, at the beginning. But we brought you to us, and put you into this form, as an infant, and raised you as our own. Because we loved you. And in this form you shall remain. That was the price we paid. We gave up your shapeshifting capacity to let you be who you are. And to keep you away from him. You may be ready one day, but you're not yet."

"We don't *have* time to wait for the perfect moment," said Jax. He leaned forward and kissed her cheek. "You've been the best mother. But time has run out. I know this. And if you think down into it, you know it too."

He sent her everything he had—the love, the loyalty, but also the data. The data on warming and the data on what the Cold added to it—the projections from the climate scientists, the acid levels in the ocean water, the rising sea levels—

"Stop," she said finally. "You're risking your life, Jax. And not only yours. If he turns you, it'll get worse. Because then you'll be working for him."

"There is no worse," Jax told her, "if everything's already ruined."

And he let go of her hands. He turned and screened himself mentally from her—he could bring up a good screen, even from his mother, now. She couldn't get into his mind; she couldn't even see him.

"Jax? Jax!" she cried, stepping back. "Come back! Jax? Where are you?"

She waved her arms in front of her like someone newly blind, trying to find him with touch. She stepped around like someone dancing, trying to run into him.

But it didn't help her, and the portal was already opening.

"That's weird. I don't see Jax anymore," said Hayley, gazing out the window. They'd closed the door, though they were still waiting for the other two, to keep the warmth inside.

Cara saw her mother turning around and around, her arms stuck out, her mouth moving. She couldn't hear over the sound of the rotor, of course, but she could tell she was talking—and she looked panicked.

"I can't," she said. It felt wrong, suddenly, to be inside and warm. And on the brink of leaving Jax. She unclicked her seatbelt and rose, grabbing the door's lever.

"Wait—what?" said Hayley. "What are you doing?"

"I can't let him go," Cara told her. "Not by himself. But you stay. Please. You've done so much, Hay. Stay. Be safe."

And she jumped out onto the rocks again, running up behind her mother; she grabbed her arm.

"What's going on?"

"He's screened himself," said her mother, shaking her head. "I can't break through it. He's about to do something so dangerous—maybe he'll listen to you! He won't listen to me. I sense there's a portal opening, but I can't see it—I don't know where it is—call out to him, won't you?"

She could do better than that. She closed her eyes and summoned. *Show me where Jax is.*

And there was another portal, like a blazing ring at the far end of the island—a ring through which she could only see darkness. Before she opened her eyes she noted the exact position of its borders—on the left, a rock with a white surface; on the right, a black rock with a sharp peak.

"I love you. I have to go with him," she told her mother.

She didn't let her eyes rest on her mother's face; it was too upsetting. Instead she was running and holding her breath; she put her arms up in front of her face against the fall, and as she leapt into the air between the two rocks, her legs bicycling, she called out her little brother's name.

———

He heard her before he saw her, spinning around in the dark heat of the cavern—his eyes hadn't adjusted yet—and then, even more surprisingly, heard a second voice too, another female one, and anxiety spiked: their mother must have followed.

But after a few seconds light flooded the chamber. Their mother hadn't come: instead, behind Cara was Hayley.

He shut the portal swiftly and stared at them.

It was Hayley holding the light—or rather making the light. It flowed from her hands, which she held up in front of her.

"You weren't supposed to *come*," he told them angrily. It actually scared him, to see them here. He was nervous for himself, even anxious, but for them he was *scared*.

"I had to," she said. "Jax! I couldn't let you come all by *yourself.*"

"Yes, you could," he said. "This wasn't what I *wanted*. At all. You can't *help* me. Don't you see?"

If he'd left the portal open long enough to compel her back through it, their mother would have made it in too—and that was more than a headache. His mother had talents Cara didn't; she *might* have been able to stop him. She'd been about to try, he knew. And then he might have had to compel her, and that would have damaged both of them. He could open a second portal now, right back to the Institute, but he didn't want to compel Cara either. If he compelled his sister—his closest ally and friend in this world, he admitted—she'd never trust his mind again.

Although in this case it might have been worth it. She might have hated him for it, or hated his memory, if he failed. But at least she would have been safe.

"I can't protect you, and trying will only hurt me," he said. If that didn't convince her, nothing would. Plus it had the advantage of being true. "This isn't a place for kids."

"Ha," said Cara. "Says the eleven-year-old."

"But I'm not eleven, as it turns out. Not really."

"I get that you're a genius," said Cara. "I respect it. So much, Jax. More than I can say. But you still have nightmares. And sleep with a blankie."

"He does?" asked Hayley.

"I'm not really eleven," he repeated dully. "But forget that, I don't want to argue. I'm asking you, please. Let me send you back to Thrace. Now. Before he gets here. *Please.*"

He was hugging her exactly as his mother had begged him—and, he saw, just as uselessly. They were equally stubborn. He shook his head.

"Um, so where *are* we?" asked Hayley.

He kept shaking his head. He was so mad he didn't want to talk to them.

"Come on, Jax. We're here now," said Cara. "So you better tell us what we're supposed to be doing."

"We're beneath," said Jax.

"Beneath what?" asked Hayley.

"Beneath it all. Beneath the water, beneath the sand. Deeper than people have ever been. Inside the rock of the Earth's crust."

"Wow. Well, at least it's warm," said Hayley. "I was afraid we were going to be frozen again."

She let the light fade from her hands a bit. They could see the walls of the cavern better now, chunky with rock and not quite stable—they were moving, like magma. But their eyes were growing used to the dark, and her light had become distracting.

"The oxygen won't last," he said. "It's going to get hard for you to breathe."

"And you," said Cara.

"He wants me," said Jax. "But he has no use for you. You're like mosquitos, to him."

"No, not mosquitos," said a voice.

Jax swiveled and looked all around. Nothing.

"Mosquitos are with me," it said. "Mosquitos are my friends. Malaria. Yellow fever. Dengue. Elephantiasis. Zika. West Nile. Tularemia. Chikungunya. Mosquitos are my friends. And yours, Jackson. We don't need homo sapiens. What are they but a scourge?"

"Show yourself," said Jax.

"Are you ready to see me?"

"Show yourself," he repeated.

The truth was, he wasn't ready at all. He'd never be.

But this wasn't about him.

At first she couldn't tell what she was seeing. There were too many shadows. Shapes blurred. She rubbed her eyes and thought about calling up a vision—maybe, now that she had a little experience, her mind could see clearer than her body.

But then *she could* see.

Something stood around Jax—around him and almost within him. Yes, within *him*, because it and Jax weren't two different beings, not entirely. They were like a Venn diagram: they intersected with parts of *themselves*, while parts were separate.

The part that was outside Jax was more fluid, shifting and changing as it spoke. At first it had tentacles, then fins, then wings; one moment it was darkly opaque, the next it was translucent.

"Take your physical form," said Jax. "I know you have one. You had to have one, to be my father. Coward."

"*Coward*," said the voice, mocking. "You think I rise to human bait? You think I'm as simple as they are?"

"It's a request," said Jax. "Not an order. Not a taunt. I want to see you as my mother did. My biological mother. She believed you could change. Or so they tell me."

"Love," mocked the voice. "A human conceit. Biology dressed up in delusion. It'll take more than that to entice me. Your mother was stupid, like all her kind. She belongs to a slave race. That's all your people are good for."

"Slaves rise up," said Jax. "Slaves always will."

The voice laughed—a huge, ricocheting noise that bounced around them. This was an echo chamber.

"I'm not impressed, boy-child," it said. "You're playing games. All I want is myself. For you *are* myself. I made you, and I can unmake you. You belong to me."

"Then show yourself," said Jax. "I want to know who I belong to. I'm *not* stupid."

The dark shape paused in its movement, and then it shrank and started to coalesce.

"I can look like anything," it said. "So could you, once. Before they stole that from you. Who do you want me to be?"

"I already told you," said Jax. "Now you're acting stupid. I want you to be my father."

"This?" said the voice.

And it lost its translucence. And was their dad. Complete with glasses and suit and vest. Looking like the fuddy-duddy he was. Cara felt a surge of fondness, of missing him, despite herself.

"I meant my biological father," Jax said. "As you well know. Not the one I know."

"I am here," he said. "As you wished. Now watch what I do."

And the form that looked like their father grew thin and pale, blood leaking from his eyes and rising through his skin. The form crumpled and fell. Something black rose from him again.

"Too small for human sight," said the voice from the black. "My scale is not your own. Your eyes are no match for me."

"Then since our eyes can't see you, use our words. Tell us your *name*," said Jax. He was shivering, Cara saw, despite the warmth of the cavern. "What is the name we give to you?"

But Cara had the sense he already knew.

The blackness rose up and loomed over them. It had the shape of a skull, vaguely—or no, it shifted again and now it had the shape of a massive horse's head, but with sharp teeth. Holes where its eyes should be.

Hayley clutched Cara's arm.

"My name is Virus," it said, now very soft. "I live in many forms. Not one. And you have no cure for me."

Jax stood silent for a long moment.

"Join me, boy. You can lead my army. We can own this world. Choose victory. Not death."

"There *is* no choice," whispered Jax, and raised his arms.

It looked like surrender.

"Jax! No!" yelled Cara, but he was already speaking.

"I call to you," said Jax. "Elements of the earth. Ancient beings. You whose bodies have been debased. Come now. Stand up to him."

And the walls around them started to hum with a sound not unlike music. Out of them stepped figures—figures vaguely like people, but not people. Slimy and dark, with glints of bone in them.

The voice roared and its shadows shrank and turned into a million tiny beings like insects. They skittered across the floor, swarming over the children's feet—Cara's and Hayley's, not Jax's. Cara shrieked as they began to climb up her, shrieked and stamped, trying to knock them off. Beside her Hayley was turning around in circles, a blur of panic.

"Not your death, fool," screamed the voice. "Theirs. You're choosing to kill them! Say yes to me and I will let them go!"

"Bind him," Jax was shouting, and around him the black things swirled like a tornado, not touching him. "Take him down deep! Take him into the burning lakes!"

"Murderer," said the voice. "Son. Murderer. You're just like me."

In the chaos Cara knew she was getting sick, terribly sick. The tiny black creatures were burrowing into her skin—burrowing into Hayley's, she saw through her tears, making holes in her clothing, splitting the skin on her fingers. And now they were on Jax too, rending his clothing into strips. Tearing at the bare skin of his legs. She couldn't stand it. All of this was her doing—from the first day she had brought Hayley in last summer, brought Jax. He was a true genius. He had a bright future ahead of him. She knew it.

And how she loved him. *My baby brother*, she thought.

Show me the way out of this, she begged, *show me how to save them. I'd give up my life. I'd give up my life for them.*

And then the walls opened completely, rocks blowing open and crumbling, and into their midst raged a giant creature—like a dragon. But there had never been dragons. Dragons had never been. Its outlines were hazy in her blurred view. She wasn't sure what she was seeing.

"You dare to take my children from me?" roared the beast.

Could it be—was it their mother, shifted?

Cara was on all fours now, half-blind. But it couldn't be their mother, she thought, more and more confused. This form was like a dinosaur. Her mother couldn't shift like that—only the forms she'd known, she had told Cara once. Only the animals of the modern world.

246

There was only one shifter who could do this, more ancient than the rest: Q.

The creature raised itself up and came crashing down, surrounded by the black figures of the earth that Jax had called, and all of them together fell upon the moving mass that was the Cold. They enveloped him.

And then Cara collapsed on the rock, arms and legs caving in, the muscles weak as paper.

It was so dark here, but not bad. Dark and soft like a dream.

Deep, deep, deep. They had sunk through the floor with their charge, and down they moved—he felt it, the knowledge a parting gift from them. They were taking his father somewhere from which he could never rise again. Revenge.

The elements of the earth had been his father's tools, but not anymore.

And it was the best he'd ever felt, that knowledge. For a second he was light as air. For a second, too, he had a memory of who he'd been before—a flying thing, a swimming thing, anything. He had been anything, once, that he wanted to be . . . and then he left that life, and he was only human.

So now there was pain, and there was death. Solid reality. He was with the others. He sat up and glanced down at himself. He was bleeding and torn, but he was whole.

Hayley and Cara lay near him, crumpled on the floor. He dragged himself over to his sister on his scraped-up arms.

"Cara! Cara!"

She was so still. And on her face were tracks of blood, like tears that had dried.

No, no, he pinged, but her mind was out of reach. As though it wasn't there at all. As though it was simply gone.

"Jax?" mumbled Hayley, and rolled over toward him.

"I can't find her," he said desperately. "She isn't here...."

He heard a groan from behind him and spun. The great beast lay there, taking up most of the space. It was harder to breathe now, he realized. He had to draw the breaths deeper. He stood and walked to the ancient beast, their great ally and friend. More than that.

He knew her now.

"Take your true form," he said gently. "So she can see you before you have to go."

And the beast shrank and shrank until she was human again. Hayley gasped and struggled to stand, running over to her and kneeling down beside her, touching her hair.

"My little girl," whispered her mother. She turned her face and looked at Jax. "My little boy."

All these years, all his talents, all his data, and this most vital fact he'd never known. He hunched beside her, alongside Hayley, and took her hand.

"What great things you've done," she whispered, even more faintly. "What great things you *will* do."

And she lifted the hand Jax wasn't holding and extended it toward Cara's body. A soft light rose from it.

"Here," she said. "The last thing I can give you."

Ten

For Cara the helicopter flight didn't even last a minute. When she and Jax and Hayley limped through Jax's last portal to the rocky island, everyone was too exhausted to talk, and their mother's anger at Jax was defused by her relief. Cara was too tired to worry and passed out in the red chopper right away, her head slumped against Hayley's shoulder.

She didn't wake up until they were landing on Thrace's roof. "The portal tech is for emergencies, typically," she heard her mother telling Max and Zee as they went inside. "What you *didn't* know was, there are risks. . . ."

When they entered the great library it was crowded and silent. Then a cheer went up for all of them as though they were heroes; but Hayley was still in shock, and none of them could forget their last sight of Mrs. M.

After she made Cara well again she'd dwindled, her familiar body on the floor dissolving into patches of light. The light had seemed to direct itself, Cara remembered as they passed through the crowd, as it faded, seeping into Hayley and into Jax and then disappearing entirely.

Her name became a whisper in the crowd. Q. Q. And then it was a chant, solemn and reverential. Q. Q. Q. Q.

Cara had one of Hayley's hands, and Jax had the other. She was their sister now, Cara thought. No: she always had been.

The crowd parted for them, and there were the old ladies—Trudy at the head of them.

They looked so sad.

Trudy reached out for Hayley's hands, which Jax and Cara let go of so that she could take them.

"We were your mother's flock," she said gently. "We've followed her—oh, for centuries now. She always gave herself. She always healed. And she always fought selflessly, whenever she was needed. We loved her most deeply. And deeply we mourn her loss."

Hayley's face was down. She nodded miserably.

"But you should know, she always knew this day would come. She lived to protect you—you, Hayley, and you too, Jax. Your half-brother, Hayley. She had the gift of foresight. She had lived a long, long time. But for all the time she lived, she never had children before you two. Her duty lay elsewhere. You were the gift she gave herself after all the struggle, all her long years protecting our people. *You* were what she always wanted. A child who could live a human life—then two of them. It was what she wanted for Jax too, despite all his abilities. A human life. And she was ready to give her own for you. To know that in the giving, you would be safe. Or as safe as any child can be."

Cara saw that Hayley was crying. Maybe she was coming out of shock.

"Can I—I want to be alone a bit," said Hayley, through her tears. "Maybe with Cara. Or Jax. But not—can I just be alone a bit?"

"Of course," said Trudy. "Shelley. Take them to a private room. And Hayley, remember. She'll always be with you. She's not gone. She's in you. And she always will be."

"The light," whispered Cara. She hadn't meant to say it out loud, but she did.

Jax, walking behind the other three down one of the wood-paneled hallways, was feeling not victorious, not proud, but heavy with a great weight.

It was the earth that had subdued the Cold, not him. He'd only signaled to the ancient bodies. He'd known they had it in them, while the Cold had assumed they were his, forever and only. He'd felt entitled to them.

But in the course of it he'd almost killed his sister. He'd almost killed both his sisters.

His father had been right: he *was* a murderer. He had it in him. He would have sacrificed all three of them to put the Cold where he belonged, to stop him.

Yes, it had been for a cause. A cause that was bigger than a few small individuals.

But wasn't that how bad guys always justified their actions?

They came to a door carved with leaves and branches: the image of an oak tree. Shelley opened it and stood holding it for the girls, who filed in past him. Then he was looking at Jax out of his big, dark eyes.

Hero, he pinged. *Not villain.*

"Thank you for reassuring me," said Jax aloud. He

shook his head. "I appreciate your kindness. But Shelley. Tell me. What's the difference?"

Intention, pinged Shelley.

"No. Everyone thinks their intentions are good."

Don't be an idiot. You saved many. Many, many, many. Today you saved multitudes.

"But I could have gotten my sisters killed," said Jax. He didn't mind if Hayley and Cara heard him from inside the room—they had a right to know. They did know, anyway. They'd been there. They'd felt disease creep into them.

Know this, Jackson: your sisters were also willing to die for you.

It was the same room she'd been in last year, which now felt like a lifetime ago—a bedroom whose walls were covered with portraits of both animals and people.

They meant something different to her now. These were the friends of Thrace, down through the ages. Or at least the more recent ages.

"I know this room," she told Hayley softly. "Do you want—do you want to lie down? You must be so exhausted. You didn't get any sleep in the helicopter, did you? Do you want to sleep now?

Hayley shook her head.

"I can't. I'm too—I don't know what to feel. But I can't sleep. I can't believe it, Cara. That Jax is—and *she* was—I can't believe she's not—I can't believe she's gone. My mother—Cara. Is it true?"

"She did it to save *you*. It was what she wanted. You heard what Trudy said."

Cara put an arm around her shoulders and guided her over to a loveseat that looked like it could have been in the court of some long-dead king—a high back, clawed feet like on an old bathtub, and a pattern of green and gold diamonds. They sat down on it next to each other. Jax was still talking to Shelley at the door—sounding like a one-sided conversation, since Shelley's part was pinged.

"I keep thinking I'll go home, and she'll just be there. Like she always was. Popping her gum. Acting like the normalest mom in the world."

"I know," said Cara. "I never, in a million years, would have thought she was part of this. That she was Q. A healer. Your mother was an amazing person, Hay. And she was always looking out for us. Her and her old ladies, getting their wash-and-set. Getting their helmets of white hair made—well, purple."

Hayley giggled through her tears.

"Where will I go, Cara? Where will I even live?"

"You'll live with us, of course."

"But your father doesn't even *like* me."

"Of course he likes you."

"He thinks I'm a 'woman of little virtue.' Remember when he said that?"

"About your skinny jeans. I remember. He was just teasing. We're sisters. That's a silver lining. Isn't it?"

Hayley nodded and wiped the corner of one eye.

"I always wanted us to have a big family. Like you do."

"I know she would have wanted it too. She gave Jax to my parents partly to hide him, but partly because she knew they would love him and take care of him. She'd want the same for you. I know she would."

Hayley nodded again.

The door shut; Jax stood there awkwardly, his face downcast.

For a time they were all silent. Cara felt the strangeness of living in a world where someone dear had died. She couldn't imagine how it felt to Hayley.

I'm so sorry, he pinged. *I hope one day you can forgive me.*

"Jax," said Cara. "*We* followed *you.* You did what you had to do."

"I don't blame *you,*" said Hayley. It occurred to Cara that she thought Jax was talking about their mother—not the two of them. And partly, he was.

For putting you in danger like that. And for Q.

"Look, she's a grownup," said Hayley. "I mean. She was. She made her own decisions. You're just a kid."

Jax shook his head.

"Get over yourself," added Hayley.

She got up from the sofa and walked over to an ornate mirror on the wall.

"My eyeliner is chaos," she said. "Why didn't you tell me I looked like a Goth in a rainstorm? Geez, guys."

And she was wiping her cheeks off with her finger.

Jax and Cara looked at each other.

"I can't believe you still sleep with a blankie," went on Hayley.

"*Some*times," said Jax defensively. "Before our mother came home."

"We're going to make some style changes for you," said Hayley. "A full-on nerd makeover. I can't be having a baby brother who sleeps with a blankie when he's already eleven. Plus, there's your clothing issue. The T-shirts with the supposedly witty sayings about Albert Einstein? They're going to have to go. *That will not stand.*"

"Well. I'm glad to see you're back to your old self," said Jax.

She turned from the mirror and looked at him fiercely.

"I'm *not.* I'm *not* back to my old self, Jax. Because my old self had a mother. My dad—I mean, you know. He hit her. He kicked *me.* When I was so little . . . it was always her and me. It was always just the two of us. And now there's only one. So I'm not my old self. And I never *will* be."

"I'm sorry. I meant—"

"But for right now I'm going to act *as if.* The way she'd want me to. Get it?"

"Yeah," said Cara. "I think we do."

"So . . . this room is boring. Can we get out of here? And where's my bag? Did someone, like, steal our possessions in all of this crazy mess? I wouldn't put it past Shelley. That ape steals guns. Maybe he steals kids' purses too. I need my phone. And my hairbrush. And my cherry chapstick."

"Probably back in the library, I'd guess," said Jax.
"Then let's go," said Hayley.

The somber tone that had governed the room when they left
it had vanished. Instead there was now a massive celebration taking place. Loud music played, some of it a kind Jax
couldn't remember hearing before—he'd research it one day.

And on the wall, where before the great portal had been,
was a vast picture of Q. Mrs. M. His first mother.

But it wasn't a static image; it moved through some of her
different forms—the forms of dinosaurs, pterosaurs, strange
mammals, insects. He saw a coelacanth, even a trilobite.

"But she wasn't *that* old," whispered Cara. "Not by a
long shot. Right? So how did she shapeshift into that?"

"She could take forms not only from what lived concur-
rently with her, but from anything that ever did. But it was
an act of imagination, not genetics. I mean it had nothing
to do with DNA. Anyway, we don't have any legitimate DNA
samples older than a few hundred thousand years, so something like the scenario in that dumb *Jurassic Park* movie
is flat-out impossible. DNA molecules degrade, see, in an
exponential decay process. Some models have it decaying to
one base pair after 6.8 million—"

"TMI," said Hayley. "Imagination. Got it. You should
have stopped right there."

There were other pictures around them on the walls as
well, both animals and people, fading in and out and being
replaced by different ones.

"Those are the others who fell today," he told them. "Even the old ways can't bring back the dead."

This was the way the old people grieved: they had parties and danced. They played music and laughed.

He liked it better than a funeral.

They stood there for a long time watching the walls.

I was almost up there, thought Cara. *My picture*. Instead, Q/ Mrs. Moore was gone. And she wouldn't come back. Not this time.

"She lived the life she wanted to live," said her mother, appearing beside her and slipping an arm around her waist.

"I thought you weren't a mindreader," said Cara.

"I just know what you're thinking," said her mother, and put her arm around her. "Now and then."

They walked a few steps away from the others.

"So maybe it was out of line, but I told Hayley," she said to her mother, "that she's going to live with us. From now on."

Her mother smiled.

"That was always our agreement, her mother's and mine."

"But . . . what will we tell dad?"

"We'll tell him the truth," said her mother. "I'm looking forward to it."

"It's going to blow his *mind*," said Max.

He and Zee had come up on her mother's other side.

"It will," agreed their mother. "He won't think about his work for almost a whole day. I guarantee it: for a period of at least twenty-four hours, he will completely forget about the flagellants."

Oh my God, thought Cara. She'd completely forgotten.

"Courtney!" she said. "Courtney!"

She couldn't possibly have slept through all this. Where was she? What was she thinking?

"Courtney," said her mother. "Yes. Luckily for you, they told me she was here when I got out of the infirmary. We made sure she kept sleeping. And Mr. Sabin took her home. When she wakes up, she'll think she had the craziest dream of her life . . . but not too long afterward, she'll find out her father is in a military prison in Connecticut. She'll need her friends then."

"We'll totally help her deal," said Hayley. "I have experience with deadbeat dads. I'm on it. Fully."

Jax couldn't see Cub anywhere, so he left the great room and went to find him.

Sure enough, he sat in the otherwise empty deepscreen room, engrossed in the computer.

"Cub," said Jax, and put a hand on his friend's shoulder.

Cub didn't turn from his screen.

"This is so wild," he muttered. "You weren't lying."

"Of course not," said Jax. "Er . . . lying about what?"

"About the ETs," said Cub. "About the aliens. In our midst!"

"Yeah, no," said Jax. "Told you."

It wasn't the right moment, he guessed, to mention that he was one of them.

"This tech is amazing," said Cub. "It never could have come from earth. Their whole system—it's not even based on binary!"

"Hey. Why don't you take a break and come with me?" asked Jax. "I'll let you look more some other time. Right now there's a—well, I guess it's a party. A celebration. Because we won, Cub. We suffered losses, but we won. For now. And you were part of it."

Cub spun around on his swivel chair, adjusted his glasses, and grabbed his laptop.

"I'm in."

As they walked out of the deepscreen room the lights dimmed into darkness behind them.

"I was thinking," Cub said. "You know that whole grade-skipping thing?"

"Yeah," said Jax. He'd forgotten all about it, but now he was reminded. There was always something to be bummed out about.

"So I'm thinking I'll just say no," said Cub.

"But they won't listen. You told me yourself. They never do."

"Worst case, I actually just go to classes with you. I just won't go where they want me to. Like, civil disobedience. What are they gonna do, arrest me? For peacefully pro-testing? But I'm hoping it doesn't come to that. You said it yourself, I just helped save the world. From an evil alien. If I can't take on my parents, well, who could?"

"Go for it," said Jax, and raised his hand for a fist bump. Cub missed it, though.

"I always acted like they had the power. I'd say no, but I wouldn't really put up, like, a fight. I'd just keep my head down and wait till they stopped talking. And then go to my room and shut the door. And do SETI or whatever. But this time I *will* put up a fight. I mean, it's my life. Isn't it?"

"Your life," said Jax. "Not theirs."

He was smiling as they walked into the party.

⚔

It was beyond sad picking up Hayley's stuff from her house. Even though the old ladies from the salon were there—the monster hens, as Hayley still called them—and they helped out a lot, it was still hard on Hayley.

She and Cara sat in their new, shared bedroom afterward looking through the stuff they'd brought over. Jax came in eating a bowl of cereal to watch them.

"The postcards from our—from the fridge," said Hayley. "OMG. I never bothered to notice the postmarks on them. Or the addresses. I only looked at the pictures. Well, sometimes I read the words . . . just thanking her. That's all they ever said. These things are, like, *ancient.* Not ancient like my mom was, but look. This one that's from Constantinople? It's addressed to her at some other place, someplace in Minnesota. It says *1906.* Like, who even knew they had *postcards* back then."

"Constantinople should have been a tip-off," said Jax, his mouth full. "If you hadn't got a C- in history. It stopped being called that back in the 1920s."

"And Petrograd," said Hayley. "That's really old too. It says 1918 on it."

"It was Leningrad after that," said Jax. "And then St. Petersburg. If I have to give up my Einstein T-shirts, you should give up being so lame at school. *You* could embarrass *me*."

Their dad had been told the story the morning after they came back—their mother had prepared him, but then they'd all sat around the dining-room table and told him their own versions, so he wouldn't think she was crazy.

For the two days after that he'd walked around in a daze, muttering. Cara had been afraid *he* was crazy. That they'd sent him over the edge.

But then he'd gone back to the book he was writing. And she realized he always walked around the house mumbling. Just usually it was about religious history, not Neanderthals and aliens.

Sometimes he'd pop out with a sudden question, in the middle of a meal or while he was shaving. "So—your little brother can read minds. But he won't read mine unless I let him. Right?" She reassured him. Or: "You say the bad guy—his name was Venom?"

"No, Dad," said Jax to that one, patiently. "Venom's a villain in the *Spiderman* movies."

"Ah, he said he was a virus. Of course. Catchy."

Then he shambled back into the bathroom, shaving foam giving him a white beard.

The most personal thing Hayley had from her mother was scrapbooks—Mrs. M had been way into scrapbooking. There were a couple of recent ones, mostly pictures of Hayley and a good many of Jax as well, with floral borders and stickers all over them containing cute baby sayings, funny quotes from Hayley when she was younger, for example.

But the rest were older, some of them very old indeed. There were boxes and boxes.

"I'm going to keep them for later," said Hayley. "It's too much for right now."

"I think that's wise," said their mother. "Maybe when you're older, even."

She took Hayley to a storage unit she had rented for her, and they put the boxes inside. Hayley had her own key, though their mother kept the other one in case she lost it.

The only problem with sharing a bedroom with Hayley was closet space. Hayley had a lot of clothes. They started by splitting the closet down the middle, but that didn't even last a week: soon Hayley had taken over three-quarters of the rack space, then four-fifths.

"You're edging me out," said Cara. "Look. There's nowhere to even put my clean laundry."

"What can I say?" said Hayley. "You need to get some fresh outfits."

"Uh, I don't think that would solve it," said Cara.

"It's not my fault I like to have choices," said Hayley. "You're blaming the victim."

Eventually they solved it by giving Hayley the extra space in Jax's closet—which she took over entirely.

Courtney was doing pretty well with her father's court-martial. She said she liked him better when he wasn't there, and her mother, once she recovered from the "social humiliation," as she put it to Courtney, was going to meetings.

"I'm not sure what the meetings are," said Courtney. "Like, women whose husbands are criminals or something? Or like, in jail? But she sure likes them. She brings home people she never would have *talked* to before. Much less set out watercress sandwiches for. It's actually kind of awesome, hearing them talk about their husbands in our living room and using four-letter words. Yesterday this woman from Chatham, who has face tattoos, said her boyfriend was a 'douchebag.' I looked at my mother, thinking she'd be all uptight and horrified, but she was smiling this secret smile like someone had given her a service award."

They went out with Courtney for ice cream and told her about Jaye, who was coming home soon. Jaye would like Courtney, they thought. Who wouldn't? She was likable.

And they took her with them on bike rides. One day they stopped along the bike path and parked their bikes outside the hair salon.

"Time to pay the hens a visit," said Hayley.

"Hens?" asked Courtney.

"Oh. It's, like, a pet name for the ladies that run my mom's salon these days."

"Not much of a pet name," said Courtney. "Geez."

263

"Believe me, they earned it," said Cara.

Inside, the salon was busy with tourists. Cara had never seen it so busy. Trudy stood at the desk in front; the other ladies were working on haircuts and dye jobs.

"Whoa, Trudy, business is booming," said Hayley when they went in, the little bell ringing on the door behind them.

"We like to keep busy," said Trudy, and leaned in close to whisper: "Your mother was more . . . selective in her clientele."

And she nodded her head toward a picture on the wall, a picture that had never been there before: Shelley dressed as Napoleon. He had one hand shoved inside a white vest and was wearing a dark blue jacket with gold on the shoulders.

"He's really into the paintings-of-famous-people thing," said Cara.

"I had a dream with an ape like that in it," mused Courtney. "You guys know a pet ape?"

"Well. He's not really pet material," said Cara. "But we did meet him once. Yeah."

"What is that, a wig? Or gel in his hair?" asked Hayley.

"Well, that hair wasn't actually *our* work," said Trudy. "That's an *homage*. I mean, don't get me wrong, we've always been able to do hair. We mostly came in for the conversation, back in the day. But your mother—specialized. Her clients were ninety percent"—she glanced sidelong at Courtney—"well, you know . . . *old* people."

"We get it," said Hayley.

"But we've thrown open the doors to all kinds," said Trudy. "We're turning a steady profit. 'Course, this is the high season. Come winter, we'll have to advertise."

"Looks like you have plenty of young people now," said Courtney politely.

In fact there were only two clients in the chairs who didn't have gray hair. But it was a nice try at a compliment, Cara thought.

"I'd like to get an ombré," said Hayley. "You know, just color on the ends?"

"I may be a thousand years old, but I do know what an *ombré* is," said Trudy.

"Hot pink, I think."

"Now, Hayley," said Trudy. "You know she never let you dye your hair."

"Hey, I was just a kid then," said Hayley. "She'd let me *now*. Don't you think?"

Trudy cocked her head, considering.

"Well, maybe just an *ombré*," she said. "We can always trim it off if you decide you don't want it. Here. I'll make you an appointment."

"Where is Shelley these days?" Cara asked her. Weirdly, she kind of missed him.

"He's taking a trip home to see some family in Borneo," said Trudy. "When he comes back, he claims he's going do some educational filmmaking. How did he put it? *Major YouTube videos.*"

Jax was taking Elvis for a lot of long walks these days. The walks let him think in solitude—about the father and mother he hadn't known so well, the father and mother he did. About what would come next.

Max had given him Puppy's naming rights, and Cara had told him what Mrs. M had suggested. So he named Puppy Elvis in her honor.

"All animals loved Mrs. M," he'd told Max. "They practically worshipped her. Did you know that no shapeshifter ever takes a dog form? Dogs are apart. They're special. Some treaty was made with the wolves long ago, and a subset of old-way people took wolf forms and split off from the wild wolves and began living with humans. So all dogs are part old-way people. And part wolf, of course."

"Yeah. The second part I knew," said Max.

"All they have left of the old-way talents is a little mind-reading. And the gift of loyalty."

"Jax," said Max, and looked at him earnestly over the top of his mug (he'd taken up drinking coffee). "I hope you never stop teaching me stuff."

It was one of the best things his brother had ever said to him.

About the Author

Lydia Millet (lydiamillet.net) is an American novelist and
conservationist. *The Bodies of the Ancients* is the third in
her Dissenters series for younger readers, following *The
Fires Beneath the Sea* and *The Shimmers in the Night*. Her
novel *My Happy Life* won the PEN Center USA Award for
Fiction, and she has been a finalist for the Pulitzer Prize
as well as a Guggenheim fellow, among other honors. Her
most recent novels for adults are *Sweet Lamb of Heaven*
and *Mermaids in Paradise*. She lives in the desert outside
Tucson, Arizona, with her two children and works for the
Center for Biological Diversity.